TRIAL BY NIGHT

Ghosts, or The Dangerous Fog

and

The Seduction of Perry

Two Novellas of Gay Love, Horror, Innocence, and Deception

Perry Brass

Belhue Press

Cover and interior design by Tom Saettel.
Cover photograph by Perry Brass

ISBN (10): 1-892149-35-4

ISBN: (13): 978-1-892149-35-0

Library of Congress Control Number: 2023932150

Other Books by Perry Brass

Sex-charge (poetry)

Mirage, a science fiction novel

Works and Other 'Smoky George' Stories

Circles, the sequel to Mirage

Out There: Stories of Private Desires. Horror. And the Afterlife.

Albert or The Book of Man, the third book in the Mirage series

Works and Other 'Smoky George' Stories, Expanded Edition

The Harvest, a "science/politico" novel

The Lover of My Soul, A Search for Ecstasy and Wisdom (poetry and other collected writings)

How to Survive Your Own Gay Life, An Adult Guide to Love, Sex, and Relationships

Angel Lust, An Erotic Novel of Time Travel

Warlock, A Novel of Possession

The Substance of God, A Spiritual Thriller

The Manly Art of Seduction, How to Meet, Talk to, and Become Intimate with Anyone

King of Angels, A Novel About the Genesis of Identity and Belief

Carnal Sacraments, A Historical Novel of the Future, Set in the Last Quarter of the 21st Century, 2nd Edition

The Manly Pursuit of Desire and Love, Your Guide to Life, Happiness, and Emotional and Sexual Fulfillment in a Closed-Down World

Acknowledgements and Thanks.

I would like very much to thank my husband Hugh Young, my close friend Ricardo Limon; my boyhood friend Lee Ellis; Tom Saettel; Gary DePasquale and Bill Crist; James Teschner; Jason Serinus and David Bellecci; and all the people who have given me nurturance in the pursuit of this book. And I'd especially like to thank Felice Picano who believed I should write it.

Foreword

These are two novellas, longer but basically short pieces of fiction, that deal with the heart itself, especially the "gay" heart looking for connection and finding it, as well as losing it. I say the "gay heart," but I think anyone's heart can understand these stories. Although both of these novellas are pure fiction, I can say as a writer that many of my deepest feeling are in them. But then that, of course, is what fiction is about—the deepest feelings of the writer, and the reader.

In both novellas, I appear as both a character and witness, or narrator—which is basically the role of any author, that is, you put yourself into the story, even if you are not there by name. Both novellas have a confessional aspect to them, and I enjoyed the fact that as a character in them, I will fall flat on my face many times, something that most people don't easily confess to, but writers can. At a certain point no matter how seriously you take yourself, you can look at yourself stripped of defenses, comic and indeed foolish. I hope I have gotten down to that level here, because I think it is where the most truth emerges.

The first novella was written recently, and the second one which takes place in the 1990s, is older and has gone through a number of revisions. Both stories are about innocence, how we see ourselves as innocent, even when we are not, and also how dangerously misleading the appearance of innocence can be. This is especially true when innocence is taken to be not believing in any possibility of your own guilt or culpability. We see this in what is called the "Karen" syndrome (or for men, the "Ken" one) when people, especially certain white people, are so convinced of their "innocent" entitlement that they cannot for a moment see the evil they are doing.

Unfortunately, a great deal of "p.c.ism" is involved with this kind of sanctimony and entitlement, and the first novella, be warned, does stick a sword through it.

While Sigmund Freud was quoted as saying, "Gentlemen, there are times when a cigar is only a cigar!" innocence and its appearance can have the solidity of a brick, and be so capable of working toward their own defense that they stray into the territory of total guilt and perpetration, even if no one admits it. In "Ghosts," the first novella, one of the characters protests how much he hates "drama," while of course being the origin and engine of so much of it. In the second novella, "The Seduction of Perry," drama at the very beginning of the story, is the very meat and realm of books and writers; soon we see how in rejecting a "literary" life, that is, one of deeper engagement with the mind as well as feelings, we invite a destruction and emotional flatness that can be easily filled with . . . well, let's get that out in the open: horror.

Real horror. The horror of our own daily and often unfulfilled lives.

We see this situation more and more as genuine awareness is denied and derided in our often oblivious, business-driven culture. In other words, if you don't buy the entire ticket of corporate consumerism, and you do retain your own feelings and consciousness, there is something desperately wrong with you. Something is even missing.

I hope you will find that very missing "something," here in these two novellas.

Perry Brass

Table of Contents

Ghosts, or The Dangerous Fog

The Seduction of Perry

Ghosts, or
The Dangerous Fog

It all began innocently enough—innocent for an age of Covid19, galloping inflation, brainless mass shootings, and a preening, self-laudatory culture that got a wild kick out of sticking its tiny skull up its butt, then coming back full of TV commercials, admiring the process. I had been introduced to Stephen Hong-Moore by Daniel Streep, a man I hardly saw anymore, as he had moved to Costa Rica years before. Daniel and I had been involved together in radical gay politics, back in that distant era when "Tricky Dick" Nixon was president, and kids like us marched, protested, and formed organizations with words like "Liberation" and "Activists" in them. No one was an activist anymore. They were careerists; the whole idea of giving yourself freely and completely (with no monetary compensation) to a cause was close to impossible. Rent was sky-high, and there was food for your stomach, cellphone bills to pay, car insurance, and the always lurking fear of finding oneself stone-broke on a dark Saturday night in some near-naked position of embarrassment or, worse yet, abject humiliation.

Daniel was in New York for a short visit, and wanted to come by the Byron Gardens, the place where I lived with my husband Keith, a retired doctor. The Byron Gardens sat on the steep crest of a palisade, or plateau, several stories above the Hudson River, at the western exposure of Riverdale in the North Bronx. The Gardens were picturesque, in a stony, 1920s-rusticated, "Isn't it just darling?"-Italian-village kind of way—almost intoxicatingly so—but they could be a hardship to reside in: bitter cold in the winter when the Hudson's freezing winds blasted through the high face of its surrounding cliffs, and our "Gone With the Wind"-era radiator heat cut off.

But it was a perfect day when Daniel came by, driven from his Manhattan-based sister's apartment by Stephen and his Chinese husband Larry Hong. They were a charming couple, both fairly tall and enviably handsome, Stephen pure kinetic energy all over, "oohing" from our balcony view of the New Jersey palisades at the end of summer, and Larry more thoughtful, hanging back. I was not quite ready for them, not sure what to make of them, but Streep was always endearing—lapsing into Spanish, which crawled into his head and sometimes just poked out. That made sense. I had not been to Costa Rica, but had heard how beautiful it was, the perfect place for an American gay man with a still-comfortable amount of money, which Daniel had from a family dairy-farming business back in Michigan. Daniel had a face that could be called "earthy handsome": his nose a generous smidge too big for it, but sitting beautifully with the rest of him, his skin clear and healthy, his eyes like one of those mirror-blue New York skies, the kind that easily reflect their own blue into the Hudson. I asked Stephen what he did.

"I teach American politics at Central Bronx College; I'm head of my department."

"So you must live close?" I asked.

"Nope. We have a teenager, a boy, so we wanted to live some place out where he could find a public school that accepted him. See, he's . . . 'gender non-binary.' We knew he'd be pretty much destroyed in most New York City public schools, so we did research and found a public school way out in Pennsylvania, about two and a half hours from here, that would welcome him. So we moved out there, to the country. I only come into Central Bronx twice a week, and do everything else from home. So it's a hard commute but not impossible, if you don't do it every day."

Daniel grinned.

"Stephen teaches about us a lot. You know, what we did when we were young, Gay Liberation. His kids are grande cool. They want to know about our era—us, trying to change the world."

"You did change it," Stephen said. Then he looked at me. "Perry, would you be interested in speaking in front of my class? You're articulate, and probably good with young people."

"OK," I said. I hadn't thought about doing it, but things were so contracted in my own world of writing. I mean, how many kids even read books anymore? I ran upstairs and got him several books of mine, and then signed them for Stephen and Larry "Hong-Moore." I liked that they had hyphenated their surnames, there was something impulsively romantic about it. They had been together a commendably long time I saw; still, Keith and I had never even thought about it. The idea of linking our own two last names like that seemed a bit pretentious, even ridiculous to me. But on these two younger men, it appeared perfect: this uniting of the tall, kind of earnestly corn-fed, pink-faced Stephen and his good-looking, slender Chinese husband, in this very open, public way.

It made me feel very good, like these two guys were way ahead of the future.

A few months later, I got an email from Stephen; he had scheduled a date for me to appear in front of his class. He would take me out for lunch first, at a Mexican restaurant near the school, and then we'd drive back to his office and he'd set up everything for my appearance.

By this time, I had already developed a PowerPoint slide show of my life in the early gay movement, with fading photos, flyers, and hand-outs, back when that was how information got *disseminated* (a beautiful word, certainly). We didn't have emails then, even fax machines. You cranked things out on a mimeograph or got them "Xeroxed" at your local copy shop. Keith drove me over to the Mexican restaurant, which was in another distant section of the Bronx, one a lot more "ethnic," real and working class than where I lived in wealthy, quiet-old-mostly Jewish-white-people Riverdale. After Keith drove off, and I was seated in Las Maravillas De Mexico, where no one spoke English, I suddenly smacked my head with my hand: I'd forgotten my cellphone!

How stupid! Suppose Stephen didn't show up? The place became crowded for lunch. I could barely speak to the waitress, a plump, young Mexican woman. I tried to explain I was waiting for someone else. She looked blankly at me. Finally, I held up two fingers, and she brought water and laid out places for two.

Then Stephen appeared, apologizing for being late.

"Everything happens those few days I'm here. I couldn't even get into my office—the janitors locked the door on me. I have to share an office with two other people, so I don't even get my own key!"

We had more food than I needed to eat, and Stephen talked incessantly, most of which I couldn't hear above the Spanish-language din. Then, without offering another word, he jumped up—lunch was declared over. There was a short drive to the college. I had never been on campus, which was nice, like this green oasis of academia in a teeming section of the Bronx, with a tree-filled central courtyard, surrounded by old, distinguished, academic-looking buildings. The school, Stephen informed me, had once been private, then the city took it over and melded it into its sprawling university system. At the main student office, confusion reigned: he was not sure what room he'd be given for his class.

"I need to have AV equipment!" he ordered. "There *will* be Power-Point!"

A young Hispanic woman led him to an empty room and opened it for him. He thanked her and then glowed triumphantly at me, like Hemingway-style, he had just bull's-eyed a charging elephant or something.

"OK! We're in!"

It was a large, old-fashioned lecture room, with risers of seats, and scores of desks. Students quickly piled in. I was glad that I had the PowerPoint, because I realized that winging this would have been difficult. I wasn't a teacher and wasn't used to talking in front of students the way Stephen was.

He took complete control of the class, disappearing into a guise I would not have recognized previously. He became *Dr.* Hong-Moore, his new face like an instantly shellacked kabuki mask, popped in front of the real one I'd seen in my apartment, or maybe just twenty minutes before at Las Maravillas. His voice changed in a perceptible way: he was now doing what seemed like a well-rehearsed imitation of himself as a teacher. I wondered: was he doing this for my sake? I had been in other classes, and had actually taught, briefly, when I was younger, but I had rarely witnessed a transformation as razor-sharp as this. He was not so much Jekyll and Hyde as some gay variation of a sneaky politician trying to sell himself to the kids, many of whom were not kids at all, but young working adults.

I began talking and using a computer to move the PowerPoint slides. There were pictures of us, Daniel Streep included, back in the late 1960s and early 1970s, marching in protests, organizing in meetings, looking much of the period: long-haired, earnest, young. Questions were asked. "What was it like to live in New York then? Was it super-violent like on TV?"

"Did you get paid to do political work?"

They were shocked when I informed them that we weren't paid. We did all of this out of conviction: we understood this had to be done if real social change was going to happen. I said they could do it too, but it would be harder because of the soaring expense of living in New York. Still, they could pool resources to lower costs, which we did. I could tell this answer didn't satisfy them. When your head is barely skimming water, how do you "pool resources"? But when the last question was answered, the class applauded, then Stephen approached.

"Thanks," he said, almost shockingly blankly, that mask still firmly on his face. "You can leave now. Know how to get out?"

I told him that Keith had promised to pick me up, which was good since, with the Bronx being, in fact, huge, I had little idea how to return to Riverdale. Since I had no cellphone, I asked for his. He fished into his pocket and gave it to me, but I could tell he was put out by this. He still had a lot more of the class to teach, and basically, after my initial usefulness to him, I felt like I had become a nuisance.

I waited outside for Keith to pick me up on a quiet street facing a small park. The truth was I had enjoyed the class. The students were engaged, and interested in what I had to say, despite all the years between them and me, as well as differences in economics. When I got home, I emailed Stephen and told him so. He wrote back, thanked me kind of stiffly, but asked if I'd do it again for the next semester. I agreed to. The next class talk, I had less time to spend with him, we did not have lunch, but I got to see him teach more with that same mask now fitting a little looser on his face. Maybe he was just more accustomed to my being there, and he wasn't trying so hard to put that layer of shellac between us. He was definitely in control of the class, and, I could tell, popular as well. He seemed younger, like minus the gray hair, he could have been another graduate student, while at the same time maintaining a crisp line of authority that said he was still the teacher, and they were still the students, definitely.

By then I had figured out how to get back to Riverdale through city buses, and I thought this little chapter was completed. Then Covid19 struck, and I was sequestered at home like so many other New Yorkers. Stephen emailed me and asked me if I would do the same talk again, this time through Zoom, a platform I had used before. The city university system had its own dedicated academic version of it, with a specialist attached who'd get in touch with me to instruct me on its technicalities. He did, this very nice young man; but on the day of the class, I had a hard time getting connected to Stephen's virtual space, and we had to bring Nick, the specialist, in to get me "seated" at the right time and place. I was actually late. I had work to do, and had forgotten about the time, which didn't help. But the class went off reasonably well. Maybe just from the fact that I was more used to it.

I was now tired of doing it, and decided I was not going to do it again. I did not hear from Stephen at all, through a year of Covid, but that made sense. He was out in Pennsylvania with Larry and their "teen-ager," Jody. Since Jody was "non-binary," I recognized that they did not like to use gender-specific terms, like "son," in regard to him.

Then, with no warning, I got an email from Stephen. He told me that he was moving to Riverdale. At first, I thought he meant that he, Larry, and Jody were moving, then he explained that he and Larry had broken up.

"Covid did it. We couldn't be with each other anymore 24/7. It's not good but we decided that it was finally time for a break-up. Besides, Larry is really set on moving back to Taiwan, where his family lives. He's

7

tired of racism in America—black men getting shot by the cops. It's a good thing really. I am looking forward to being single again. I have never been single in New York! It's going to be an adventure!"

I felt immediately bad for him. I knew they'd been together for twenty-something years, and ending this could not have been as carefree as his email made it appear. I had invited him, Larry, and Jody over for dinner several times, but they never could because of the complicated logistics of their arriving together plus their distance from the city. Now I could invite Stephen alone, as soon as he moved in.

This turned out to be more difficult than either of us had imagined. The couple whose apartment he had bought in the northern section of Riverdale, close to the Yonkers line, were having a hard time moving into their next home, leading to a chain reaction of delays. It would take Stephen four months to move in, during which time he stayed with his aging mother in New Jersey, close to Philadelphia.

We kept in touch sporadically: I felt that, somehow, Stephen just had to be grieving over the relationship that he'd lost with Larry. Maybe I was simply empathizing too much, but terminating that kind of long, close relationship did feel extremely wounding to me. The idea of just cutting myself off from Keith seemed impossible, even though our relationship had taken on that kind of casual, at times thoughtless distance that long-term marriages bring into effect. You take each other not so much for granted, as forgotten. You forget who you really are: both you and he. You know there is still that young person inside him, the one you knew when you fell in love, but where is he—and what does that person actually look like now?

I mean, not the one you're with, the one who's gained all the weight—and all the years—but he is there somehow. That younger self.

Finally, Stephen moved in, and we found a weekend in early April for him to come for dinner. The question of what he'd bring became difficult. He told me that he did not eat meat, or drink alcohol—"I can bring a bottle of wine, but I don't know anything about wine. How about if I bring dessert? I know desserts!"

I told him dessert would be fine. He came with a large box of nine "bespoke" cupcakes, from a specialty cupcake bakery in New Jersey. He had traveled across the bridge to get it. They were so amazing I photographed them: each had its own gleaming, custom-flavor icing top (very *Food Channel*), with varieties like strawberries and crushed pretzels. I was impressed. Since he did eat fish, I made broiled salmon, but what delighted Stephen most was the toasted *naan* I served, drizzled with olive oil.

"I love *naan*," he said. "I've never had it with olive oil!"

I thought: that's peculiar—usually people ate *naan*, an Indian flat bread, with some kind of oil on it—but it was also peculiar that he never said a single word to Keith throughout his time that night with us. He only talked about his divorce from Larry, his work at Bronx Central, and the excitement of his brand-new life.

"I'm looking forward to being a gay *single* New Yorker," he crooned. "I'm from the Midwest and I've never really been single in New York. I was *single* in Chicago for a while, before Larry, but never here. I want to go to the bars and the baths; I'm already on Grindr!"

"How has that worked?" I asked as we figured out who was going to have which cupcake. I decided the thing to do was divide them, so we'd get to taste more of them.

He shrugged.

"It's OK. Most guys just lie to you. You do lot of stuff online—you know, 'sexting.' Then maybe they'll make a date with you; sometimes they cancel the date just before it happens. 'Sorry. Something came up.' So you go on to the next one. I am seeing this guy named Eduardo. He lives in Jersey, and is really good looking."

Stephen popped out his phone and showed me Eduardo's picture. He was indeed handsome, youngish-40s, with jet black hair and a face that invited you very quickly.

"I am really looking forward to our date."

"So, you've never actually met him?"

"No, but we know a lot about each other online. We've spent hours doing the online stuff."

I smiled, trying at least to warm up to the idea. The idea of return-ing, even momentarily, to New York's sexual gay meat market did not thrill me. As I remembered too well from being young, it could be a threatening, even vicious and dangerous place. He looked at my smile coldly, somewhat quizzically, as if stepping back and defensively asking, "What else can I do?" His expression now seemed like only another version of that shellac mask, maybe because Keith was nearby—alright, I'll give it to him—*maybe*, but all I could hope for was that Stephen was not going to get badly hurt. The kind of hurt that I remembered from my own at times difficult single days.

He emailed me afterwards, thanking me for inviting him over.

Then he had an idea: he wanted to invite Keith and me out for a Tai-wanese Sunday brunch at a special place he knew in Flushing, Queens. I asked Keith about going, and he agreed to be up for it.

But Stephen had a condition: he was still terrified of Covid. As a teacher who'd seen it cut through his class, even killing a couple of his students from poorer families, it still stalked him. Since this restaurant was a small, at times crowded, but authentic, one, we'd have to get take-out and eat everything in his new car.

Keith thought this plan was ridiculous.

"I don't eat in cars unless we're in a drive-in restaurant, and those have gone out with the phone booth."

But I thought: why not? Now I really wanted to get to know more about Stephen Hong-Moore, who still seemed a cipher to me: enthused and adolescent-crazy about Grindr sex, even with Covid-19 still lurking out there, then distant, almost iceberg cold. He was easily the popular, with-it, youngish teacher, even as he approached sixty, but I couldn't find any genuine depth in him, as much as I was willing to go deeper for it. It simply didn't seem to be findable, like I was caught up in some kind of strange, endless, adolescent Pokémon game.

But I was sure that depth had to be there. Someplace.

PART

2

That Sunday began cold, rainy, and overcast. He picked me up in his new car, a deep purple Nissan Altima, a spiffy, sporty thing, outfitted with all the newest tech bells and whistles.

I was glad to be inside, since I had waited out on the curb for him, and it was still raw, early spring weather. "I wanted *this* shade of purple in a car," he explained, "and Nissan had it. My last car was a chartreuse. I got tired of it and was ready for this purple."

I smiled. I had never met anyone who picked his car mainly by its color. Mostly at this point, it seemed that cars were either silver or black.

We were soon going over several bridges to get into Queens. Stephen drove calmly and effortlessly no matter how congested New York weekend traffic got or how crazy and aggressive the drivers acted. It was like he was still driving in the Midwest, not in our more emotionally combustive city. I looked periodically over at him, that habitual shellacked coldness still there. Finally, we were in Flushing, an outlying area of Queens that had once seemed like a little Dutch village. It was now very Asian. A large number of signs and billboards sported Chinese characters. The sidewalks were densely packed, with crowds of people smoking on them, also very Asian. The restaurant we were looking for, working-class Asian and modest, was on a dismal side street, its outside windows plastered with hand-lettered signs and pictures showing house specialties (mostly heavy on pork), but with some interesting seafood, like giant clams and big, inky seawater squid, which I liked.

Stephen managed to park, and we stood outside for a moment, looking at the window signs. Through a small gap in them, we saw that the place was virtually empty.

"I guess it's safe for us to go in," he announced, so we did. We were seated at a table next to the window. The restaurant was low lit and quiet. A very tired-looking waiter came up and handed us menus. Stephen greeted him in Chinese, and the waiter talked to him for a moment, but seemed hardly impressed at all that Stephen could speak to him. Perhaps, I thought, Stephen's Mandarin was just not that proficient.

"Do you want me to order for you?" he asked. "I've been here a number of times, so I know what's good."

I nodded. The waiter returned and Stephen said in Mandarin that we'd have a melon soup, followed by the giant clams and a pork dish for me and a fish one for Stephen that also included some shrimp with it.

Stephen beamed. "I love this place. The food's excellent—it's the food real Chinese working people eat. Larry and I went back to Taiwan often, so I spent a lot of time there. The kind of food you get in most of New York is not the kind of food they have over there. It just doesn't taste the same."

I smiled. The place seemed grubby and not terribly clean. But he was right: soon enough it did fill up with very working-class-looking Chinese or Taiwanese people. Stephen relaxed, as if forgetting about Covid.

I asked him if he'd met any new guys on Grindr.

"Yeah, and I just had my first date with Eduardo. We had the very best *anal* sex I'd ever had in my life! You just can't imagine it—he's so amazing! He can do things with his ass I didn't know any guy could do. Like he had muscles down there I didn't even know existed. I think we fucked for about two hours."

He smiled at me, like a cat that really enjoys eating a nice juicy mouse.

"Do you like him?" I asked, my eyes basically taking him in. "I mean, a lot?"

"Sure. But I don't know if we are going to have a second date. He said he'd call me, and so far, he hasn't called me at all."

"Why don't you call him?"

He paused. I wondered, was I stepping out of line to ask that?

"I dunno," he finally answered, distantly. "The truth is, I don't like going through drama with people, when things get sticky and ugly. Know what I mean?"

Actually, I didn't but just nodded.

"See, he doesn't answer his phone. I guess he screens his calls."

"Maybe he'll call you," I suggested.

"Maybe . . . a lot of these guys on Grindr, they just ghost you. They don't like drama, either. It's their problem though, not mine. The truth is I don't ghost anybody. Most of the time."

He smiled at me with that same big-cat-eating-the-mouse face. I thought: something about this situation with Eduardo must be bothering him, even if it were simply missing Eduardo's very talented ass—but he wasn't telling me.

The food came. It was interesting, but sort of second-rate Chinese food, with, I could tell, a dump-load of MSG in it. There were, though, interesting, unusual Chinese vegetables that were very fresh, and I liked that. Stephen picked them out and told me their names. He enjoyed explaining the intricacies of this type of food to me, things he had learned from years with Larry.

Jody, their non-binary "teenager," was away now in a school their son had discovered in Canada, that combined an art curriculum with technology. Stephen showed me more pictures of him on his phone. The boy was extremely handsome and quite tall.

"How did he come about?" I asked. "Was he adopted?"

Stephen shook his head.

"Larry is his biological father. His mother is my sister. She wanted to do this for us, so I'm his uncle as well as his father. The problem is Jody and I never got along as well as he got along with Larry. Maybe it's that Larry is biologically closer, but Jody was always crazy about him. I was too busy earning degrees and teaching school and having an income. Larry brought in good money; he's an operating room nurse with a PhD in nursing, but he stayed home most of the time taking care of Jody."

"How is Jody dealing with the break-up?"

He paused, suddenly the cloudy day outside passed over his face.

"Not well at all. For a time, in fact, I think he hated me. It wasn't my fault. Larry wanted the divorce. The truth is, I would have stayed with Larry for the rest of my life—I was comfortable with him. I liked that he brought with him another culture, something I wasn't used to from the Midwest. But sexually, we kind of hit the wall."

"What do you mean?"

"We stopped having sex. Larry was not into the kind of sex I wanted, with a lot of fucking and rimming, but that was OK. I can be very open about sex, but we just stopped having it completely."

"That does happen," I said. "Did you have any outside affairs, on the side?

He paused again.

I apologized to him. Maybe I was prying.

"No, it's OK. Yeah, I had these two guys I used to alternate with every two weeks. One I saw every other Monday, and another on weekends. Sometimes it was every three weeks, but they were there. I called them my Monday guy and my Sunday guy. Funny names, right? Now I can barely remember anything about them."

I got up and went to the bathroom, which was in the rear of the restaurant behind the kitchen. It was hardly hygienic at all; I wondered how this place passed health department inspections. I also wondered again what Stephen Hong-Moore was really like. It seemed to me that it would be difficult to find out without actually probing him. He put up so many barriers around himself, that shellack mask again. From our conversation, he seemed shallow, not terribly smart, and amazingly immature for someone with a PhD who had been teaching for so long.

When I returned, he announced that what he really wanted to do was go to a bubble tea place not very far away.

"Bubble tea really comes from Taiwan," he explained. "And it's spread to America. There's even a bubble tea café in Riverdale, close to where I am."

We drove about a mile through the congested streets of Flushing, that quickly resembled areas of some Chinese city I had never been to, then parked on a narrow side street somewhat near the bubble tea place. I never would have found it; it was on the ground floor of an office building, and very popular.

"They have the best bubble tea I've ever had here," he said. "It's even better than most of the tea in Taiwan."

I offered to pay for the tea, which was not cheap but very good. The "bubbles" came from flavored tapioca pearls, so it was like combining pudding with tea. I had never had it before and liked it, but more importantly loved that Stephen had really wanted to introduce me to it. He showed a special excitement out of showing me this place and telling me what to order. While I waited for our order to be made, which took a while because a number of people were waiting to be served, Stephen decided that he would retrieve the car from several blocks away—maybe out of a renewed Covid fear—and drive it up to where we were, so we'd drink the tea on the way back to Riverdale.

After I had been given the big plastic cups of tea, packed securely in a paper bag, I waited outside for him, watching multitudes of mostly young Asian people walking around me, chattering in languages I would never understand. They seemed to be very happy in Flushing. I remembered that when I had first arrived in the city, back in the mid-1960s, and was still a teenager myself, I had a job working in a large advertising agency, and one of my co-workers lived in Flushing. It was then a prosperous middle-class white area, filled mostly with Italians and Jews. Vincent, my friend, was working-class Italian, married to a very bourgeois Jewish woman who taught home economics in a high school close by. He was a talented, sort of bohemian artist; she really wanted to have kids and an idealized, suburban-TV-lifestyle kind of home. She also didn't know that he was secretly bisexual, and he soon came on to me. I liked him a great deal but was in no way sexually attracted to him.

I ventured out to Flushing to have dinner with them several times, so I got to know the area we were in. It had really changed, but so much of New York had. His wife eventually suspected that Vincent and I were having an affair, which was not the truth, but she knew that "something" was happening with her husband. The two of them broke up about three years after I met him.

I got into the car with Stephen, and he beamed at me. I told him how much I liked the tea. Suddenly he leaned over and kissed me very softly on the lips; I felt like I was going to blush all over. I had not expected it. I had wondered to myself what he was really like and—on the way home, he told me more about himself. How repressed he'd been as a tall but unathletic kid who was supposed to like basketball but hated it.

"I wanted to be making real baskets, not basketball 'baskets.' They kept wanting to put me inside some little box, and I was too tall to fit into it. It turned out that my dad was gay, but I didn't know it. After he and my mom divorced, he started seeing men. He could not really talk to me about it. He died of a heart attack when he was only fifty-three. He had smoked a lot, but I think it was the strain of keeping it a secret. That's why I never wanted to; I never wanted to keep anything a secret—we never did from Jody. He knew he was the child of two gay dads by the time he was two. By the time he was three, he had already decided he was going to be gay. He told us, 'I want to be just like you guys.' We didn't have enough money to put him into one of those elite liberal private schools, where a lot of upper-class gay and gender non-conforming kids go. So, we had to find a fairly ritzy, public school he could fit into."

He shrugged and glanced at me. I was smiling at him, genuinely now.

"It was like we didn't have a choice. Y'know what I mean?"

PART

3

During the rest of the next week, I thought about Stephen a lot, the way he had leaned over and kissed me in the car. There was something preciously intimate about it: the brief but combustive spontaneity of it, like he had been holding back that kind of affection, and now he could show it. I knew I was becoming—well, *vulnerable* to him. I didn't want to be. He was still waiting for Eduardo; I decided that.

He texted me often and I decided this time that we should do another brunch. I simply needed to see him, that was the only way to describe it. I *needed* to finish this briefly open gestalt—maybe; there were still too many pieces of the puzzle missing, and even without admitting it, I didn't want them to be. He threw several plans at me. One was that he would invite Eduardo, even though Eduardo had shown little further interest in him. And there were two other gay men who lived in Riverdale, who taught at Bronx Central, he'd invite them too. I told him it was all OK with me. I wanted him simply as my *friend*. Warmer, not quite so guarded, nor so—you know?—brittle with me. Different, from the way he'd been at the school, or even in my apartment. I would be happy with this deeper friendship, knowing he was safely situated in one of the nicer outer areas of my heart, where that kind of friendship resides.

Stephen had a plan. There was an outdoor café in Northern Riverdale where he wanted to meet. Since we were now hitting five people, it would be more "Covid-safe" to be outside. I looked up the café—the "outdoors" was simply the sidewalk with some metal chairs on it. I was not enthused about it; then on Sunday morning, it started to rain again. Stephen texted me: Eduardo could not make it—I guessed he must have answered Stephen's text, since, as Stephen informed me, this handsome guy from Grindr by nature did not answer his phone. Ditto for his two friends: no shows as well.

I suggested that he come over to my place for brunch. Keith had plans to meet with some friends to play chamber music together—Keith

16

is an amateur classical musician—and I would simply make some eggs and coffee.

Stephen insisted that he would bring bagels, then texted me how difficult it was to find bagels on a Sunday in Riverdale—the Jewish population must have thoroughly ransacked them. I told him he really didn't have to bring bagels—we had bread for toast and stuff like that. Finally, at close to three, Stephen texted me that he was in his car and on the way.

I realized I was becoming extremely enthused, very excited with Stephen, this new friend, now close-to spontaneously surfacing in my life. Even though we had known each other for a few years, there was hardly any genuine "knowing" in any intimate sense involved with it. But now he was starting to appear more solid, like some clear vision of Jupiter approaching from the very distant outer path of its orbit. Rationally, I did sort of want to keep him in that . . . OK, basically good-guy, chummy-neighbor relationship we had, since he might . . . well, fairly soon go off again just by himself. There could easily be another Eduardo. Then any closeness we'd had would probably disappear.

Spinning Jupiter, tall jovial Jupiter, completely out of my sight.

Nevertheless, I wanted him to come through the door. I wanted to listen to him talk, and just watch him. This big, Midwestern guy with a face that went from brief spurts of intensity to freak-show glassy—in other words, that shellac mask that, if truth be told, I very much wanted him to drop.

He appeared, bagel bag in hand, then dropped it at the door and grabbed me, almost crushing me in his arms. His lips were on mine; the softest lips I think I'd ever felt on a man, very soft and large and moist. I said something about them, their softness—he informed me that he had gone swimming earlier at the gym in his building. Maybe that was why his lips were so soft. I was taken so off-guard; all I wanted to do was kiss him back, just melt into him.

"You didn't expect this?"

"No."

"I've always been attracted to you. I was so attracted to you in my class I could barely hold myself back, but I was with Larry and didn't want to start anything."

"I'm attracted to you," I said, barely able to catch my breath. "I love you."

The words just shot of me; I surprised myself by saying them. I was unable to repress them.

I felt immediately terrible—I had completely surrendered to him. I felt off-balance, like you would with someone much taller; and suddenly, as if I were in some kind of fog, what the Italians call a *nebbia*, that dangerous fog of love, where reality is almost impossible to define or grasp. Love, strange and intoxicating as it is, was right there in front of me, like an escape from death; or a road driving directly into it. Suddenly I felt as if I were being fed my own *self* inflated by desire—so dangerous, so illusionary. So obviously destined to be painful. What an illusion! I wanted to hold on to him, as if in that moment he was the only thing on earth. I was crazy about him; suddenly, even against my own fucking will . . . I was *crazy* about him.

Everything else blanked out. Our clothes were coming off as fast as they could; they became a trail upstairs to the bedroom I shared with Keith. Stephen wanted to get naked so fast he didn't even take his socks off. I could not stop kissing him. We got into bed, and I couldn't stop being lost in those very soft, delicious lips. He had a large cock and was very proud of it. I am not that impressed with big cocks—I know that's kind of hard to believe, but it's true. Guys with large cocks, they—

He immediately began to fuck me, and I straddled him, then realized we'd need some lube. I got some but was wary. I had not been fucked in a long time, and did not like the risk, the unsafeness, of it.

The weird thing was that I could not get an erection. I barely found him even that attractive. I was crazy about him on this extremely deep level—that of totally unexpected, emotional surrender. Maybe it was that for this moment he had indeed dropped the mask, and I was both shocked and very pleased by it. Like we were really, stunningly naked together, even with his socks still on; he hadn't wasted a second to remove them.

I told him I hadn't been fucked in about twenty years.

I wasn't sure if that were the truth. But again, it just came out of me.

"I'm happy then that you've let me top you."

"I'm happy, too."

He noticed that I was totally soft.

"I guess this was such a surprise to you?" he said, holding my flaccid penis. I felt embarrassed, like this was not supposed to happen: I was both completely turned on by him, and yet, weirdly enough, not excited. I was still in that strangely unsettling fog, with him in it too.

He finished by coming in my mouth. I wanted to taste him: it was true. That transformation, *transfiguration of cum* from him to me—the sheer craziness of it, hitting the back of my throat and taste buds. His cum was great, almost sweet. I told him that.

"No meat in the diet," he explained. All I wanted to do was keep on kissing him; I didn't want to stop. But he held back, and suddenly we were separated again, like this gulf of frigid air had emerged between us, and there he was, floating separately in it, like a big silvery cloud.

Suddenly he came back to me.

"I was diagnosed with autism," he disclosed. "It came as a surprise to me. I mean, I knew I was"—he let go of the thought, then grabbed it again, "kind of strange. I told you I wasn't like other kids."

I became curious. I really wanted to know more about him. That must have been part of his curious attraction to me, that he had withheld so much, and now—

"What were you like in high school?"

"Total nerd. Very *un*-sexual. I repressed everything. My parents were kind of bohemian goofy. Maybe that's why I suppressed so much; I didn't want to be like them."

"I know very little about autism. I know some kids have it, but I've never met an adult with it. What's it like?"

He got up and started to dress.

"It's hard for me to say, because I'm—" he halted.

"So close to it?"

"That's it! That's why it's impossible to self-diagnose. I'm also a big extrovert. I like having people around me, sometimes a lot of them. They energize me, like I feed energy off them."

"You would have made a great politician," I said while he finished dressing. "Bill Clinton was like that. He could shake hands with four hundred people, then go into another room and shake hands with four hundred more. I would have been frazzled. Just worn out from it."

"You're an introvert, right?"

I nodded.

"Most writers are," I said. "You have to be very happy being by yourself for long stretches. If you don't like your own company, you can't be a writer."

"I like my own company. I like yours, too. We need to do this again."

I brightened when he said that. The idea of *not* doing it again already seemed torturous and impossible; for that moment I couldn't even imagine it. What we had done was so real, even if it came out of so much unreality. We went downstairs and I toasted his bagels and we had them with cream cheese and eggs. He talked some more and I listened, or pretended to listen. Just watching his beautiful mouth move with sounds of a deeper, post-sexual register coming out of it, was very satisfying to me. He talked about growing up in this small town in the Midwest where he felt gawky and queer and alone. Then he met Larry Hong who seemed so exotic and direct—with none of that bitchy, odd queerness that Midwestern faggots had—and Stephen fell for him. Larry wanted to have a child, so they did that, before a lot of other gay couples were doing it.

He got up to leave and I kissed him. Then he was gone.

A short time later, Keith came back from playing music. He told me all about the various players, their quirks and drawbacks. I barely listened. He asked me how my afternoon had gone. I told him that Stephen Hong-Moore had come over for brunch, and we had a good time talking.

"I guess he only talked about himself and his divorce and son, right?"

"Pretty much. But I like listening to him."

"That's your problem, Perry," Keith said. "You like listening too much. People take advantage of it."

I nodded. All I could think about was Stephen leaving, and how much I wanted to see him again.

PART

4

Easter was coming up, so I decided to invite Stephen over for it. We had plans to get together with two women friends, one, Gail, a musician whom Keith knew well, the other, Mary, a small lady in her eighties who lived in the Byron Gardens and was a retired dancer. Keith would have to pick Gail up at the subway, and Mary would be arriving later since she had to see her adult kids in the city for a while. Stephen texted me that being of Scottish background, he wanted to wear a kilt. I made some kind of fish dish, since Stephen would eat fish but not traditional Easter dishes like lamb or ham. Dinner was set for four o'clock. I was so excited that I went out to the sidewalk to meet him. He texted me several times about parking—being very difficult now in Riverdale, as it was in the rest of the city if not the whole world. Then I saw his tall figure cantering up the sidewalk in this outrageous rainbow-colored kilt, that seemed in its unexpected brightness very appropriate for Easter. He was carrying another large box of pastries.

The Byron Gardens had a small grove of rhododendrons growing near a narrow stone stairway down to our entrance to the apartments. He placed the box under the shrubs, then kissed me right there in front of anyone who might be walking down the street. I grabbed him and led him down the stairs to our door.

Inside, I asked, "What have you got under there?"

"Why don't you find out?"

He lifted his kilt; nothing there except his cock. I knew I only had a couple of minutes and quickly went down on him. He smiled afterwards. Then Keith arrived with Gail, a large, still attractive though talkative woman. I introduced her to Stephen.

They were quickly off to the races with tales of their respective divorces. Stephen was very proud of his—the crisp legality of it.

"It took about six weeks, and lawyers, and then I reached into my mailbox and there it was—only a couple of days before I moved into Riverdale. Now I can be what I have always wanted to be: a gay single New Yorker. I know it's a strange time to want that, with Covid, but after twenty-seven years, I'm ready for it!"

"I don't know about the gay part," Gail chimed in, "but it's not all it's cracked up to be: being single. I can tell you that."

"Yeah," Stephen admitted, more seriously. "New York doesn't even have one single working bathhouse."

Gail shot me this very funny look. "That, I can't comment on."

I had to disappear into the kitchen to finish dinner. When I returned, about half an hour later, Gail and Stephen were still talking, mostly about men and dating. Gail was in seventh heaven, like she had found a real soul mate in Stephen.

"I think we should adopt him as one of our own," she cooed. "How did you ever meet this wonderful man?"

"Through a mutual friend," I said.

"Well, you have to thank him. He's such a gentleman, and so smart."

"Thank you," Stephen said, getting up. Mary had arrived, and she introduced herself to him. I had told Stephen that she was a dancer—she still danced and had kept herself in great shape, as dancers often do. They talked very briefly together. Stephen had a small interest in modern dance, though little to say about it. Mary spoke briefly about her career. She was still teaching. The school year was winding down for both of them, and they talked about that.

Dinner was a great success. Stephen carried most of the conversation without dominating it too much. Gail was a real talker and found her match with him. Keith and I were much quieter people, and Mary who, when called on, could trot out old stories about her career, was happy, for a change, just to listen to Stephen and Gail. We opened up Stephen's box of assorted pastries, this time from another bakeshop in New Jersey, and enjoyed sharing them. And I thought: God, I want to get his clothes off again, I just want to swim again in that great tide of him.

During the week, he texted me constantly. He had met someone new on Grindr—Armand, who lived all the way in Princeton, where he was the manager of a very preppy clothing store.

"Can you believe it? I've met Mr. Right"

By now, I'd developed this idea (or survival strategy) with Stephen—that I should simply be a *good* sport. It seemed like the only possible way to deal with him and my own increasing attachment to him: namely, to enjoy his own area of the pool, even if it were an obviously shallow one—when the opportunity was offered. "Good," I texted back. "Gimme details."

"OMG where 2 begin?

"Is he Mr. Right or Mr. Right Away?"

"Mr. Right I think."

We made plans to meet on the Wednesday after Easter—Keith would be out of town playing music with friends, a weekly "play date" that amateur musicians informally arrange.

I warned Stephen by text that Con Ed was breaking up the sidewalk in front of the Byron Gardens, so parking could be even a worse pain in the neck.

He texted back: "Oh NO! Con Ed will not get in the way of our play stud."

Stephen often referred to me, and probably other men on his sex list, as "stud." That must have been a carry-over from Midwest gay slang—it would just make people in New York laugh. I mean, here everyone's a *stud* until proven otherwise. Right?

He was out by the pool of his coop. "God! I can't wait to make incredible love with you again and again sir. I better watch this or the lifeguard is gonna get quite the view lol."

"OK. Maybe he's never seen it before."

"He was staring at my crotch yesterday."

"Who can blame him?"

He sent me a raft of hearts and lips emojis, then wrote: "OK, out of the pool having lunch and then onto you as dessert sir."

5

Our Wednesday date simply amazed me; I was just dazzled by it. I had wanted it to happen so much. But it's a very easy life lesson to see that simply wanting something does not make it happen; something else has to be accomplished to make things happen. I decided that there just had to be some kind of mystic, unexplainable fire going on between us. I knew it; I felt it inside. This time, I had no problems getting hard— even though weirdly enough, on a purely physical level, Stephen didn't attract me that much. His body was too big, Jell-O-y, and soft, like one of those "beached whale" bodies you sometimes see on big men. I liked leaner bodies, and big shoulders: wide, swimmer's shoulders, a weakness of mine. Stephen did not have them, even though basically swimming was his only exercise.

Still, all of these unexplainable, wet-dream-stuff, kick-ass feelings kept spilling out of me.

It was irrational; I knew it. I couldn't stop it. I was in love with him, even against my own will. Everyone who's ever felt anything knows situations like this go on—and now I was blindly spinning, uncontrollably caught up in it.

That fog, that dangerous fog again. I felt as if I were wading right back into it, and a very deceptive undertow was swirling under it, waiting to pull me in and heartlessly drown me.

Then, without warning, he offered me a life raft.

"I love you," he said after some quiet. "I love you, too."

He had cum, then told me that. I couldn't believe I'd heard it. It seemed impossible, that I could want something so much and simply get it—then I felt his for-the-most-part, self-absorbed eyes, retracting from me, warning me of that deceptive undertow again. Was it simply waiting for me? Maybe I was just an eccentric anchor for him—and he was also in a fog of his own. I was an attractive older man who through a daily exercise-regimen kept himself in very good shape. I also had this center that writers have—this place where we connect inside with ourselves; weirdly, OK, fuckin' real weirdly, it's also a religious place. Like some dark, sacred grove of trees where men secretly go (I believe this) . . . to make love.

It's like, inside us writers there is some "religion" going on.

I wanted to taste those words "I love you, too," like I wanted to taste his cum. We all know that some word (alright *the* Word, that Word that holds everything together—call it Jesus; God; Jehovah; Shiva; Buddha; Creation; Love—that singular Word that is the-always-looked-for Doorway beyond death) . . . is

. . . *life*. Itself.

You just want to taste it, and keep it inside your own mouth, there.

Stephen seemed to have this gravitational pull towards me—or was I merely going crazy? Wasn't I the one being "pulled" by an attraction that seemed to have so little basis—I was not even physically, or at bedrock, emotionally, attracted to him?

He seemed depthless. At times stupid. He pulled out his phone, while still in bed. "This is Armand—isn't he good looking?"

He was. He looked trim and handsome, beautifully groomed and dressed.

"He's everything I've ever wanted. We sexted for ninety minutes. I've never done that with a guy!"

"So, you haven't actually met him?"

"No. But I'm going to. We're having our first date on Tuesday. That's his day off from the store. He gets Tuesdays and Wednesdays off. He's coming into town and I'm going to pick him up at Penn Station."

"I hope it goes well," I said. I wanted to say: "You're putting an awful lot of weight on this situation with someone you don't know." But I didn't. I just had to stay on that tiny-little raft he had offered me, the one emblazoned with: "I love you, too."

"I hope so too," he suddenly shot back. "One thing I'm really good at is boundaries."

"What do you mean?" I asked. Was this another part of my life raft: that he would respect my relationship with Keith, just as I would respect his with . . . well, whomever came into his life?

He became colder like someone had just shot Freon through him; that glazed mask descended instantly over his features. I watched it happen. Then he smiled, about two degrees or so warmer.

"I meant, I respect other people's time, and what *they* have to give me and *exactly* what I can give them."

I felt better. I relaxed. My dumb little life raft was still intact.

* * * * *

I texted him later: "I'm so happy you were here. You have made me really happy. I hope your meeting with Armand goes well. Enjoy it: the best is yet to come."

He sent me back an emoji of a unicorn's head with a heart next to its mouth. I figured at that point that both Armand *and* I were unicorns; you know, your basically mythical, stand-alone good guys.

Later, I texted him, "How did your first date with Armand go, or are you still on it? Been thinking about you—hope you are doing fine. Let me know how everything is going."

"Magic. Very best first date ever! Just dropped him home in NJ."

"Sounds like a 12"

[from him: Fire emoji]

I decided to dive in, or at least hold on to my raft.

"How about brunch Sunday? I have bagels."

I literally held my breath, until he texted back:

"That would be great."

I texted him that I would find out if Keith were going out to play music again. If not, we'd do "brunch" at Stephen's place. The brunch idea, or excuse, seemed fairly ridiculous, but for that moment, it seemed like a fitting way to put it.

Then I ended: "Sleep well, my Scottish Prince."

All I could think about was that on Sunday, I'd see him again. If love is an addiction, and it must certainly be, he was now standing tall at the bull's-eye center of mine. Nothing this irrational had happened to me in years. I felt a little more confident, younger, buoyant. But isn't that the way we all want to feel, especially as a never-say-die Baby Boomer recently roaring past seventy? I felt buoyant certainly, and, like I said, inflated with love. OK, maybe I simply wanted to go back into that naked sacred grove where the fun guys have cool sex: the peculiarly holy place—the writers' place—that dark, deliciously-horny realm of spectacular imaginings. I wanted to walk again into it—with Stephen; even if I had to slog through that fog to do it.

I was nuts!

As the old song goes, "Why must I be a teenager (or, seventy-plus-year-old guy) in love?"

Then on Saturday something happened.

I got another text from him:

"Change of plans. Sunday, I'm off to Harlem to pick up an Activist friend. We made plans to go to the rally at Amazon on Staten Island. Maybe we could do an early brunch from 11 to 1?"

I knew that could not work—I could not just leave Keith that early on a Sunday; besides, eating brunch was not exactly what I had in mind with Stephen. I asked if we could postpone until the next week.

What he wrote me back was incredible—I could feel that meagre "I love you, too" life raft fast gathering water, sinking by the second: Jody was returning from his year of art school in Canada. "My weekends will be full for the next 3 weeks!"

SHIT!!!

I thought my heart would stop. I felt more deflated than the value of a pork chop at an Orthodox Jews convention.

I had to do something. I grabbed for straws.

"I would love to meet Jody. Why don't the 2 of you come for lunch?" I was insane—people used to be institutionalized for life for less: I had this craving-need just to hear his voice. His text back thoroughly froze me, like an ice cube sliding down my testicles.

First, I had to get used to the fact (or convention) that, as a "non-binary," Jody was being formally referred to as "they."

"I will follow Jody's lead on who they would like to meet and when. Remember they've never seen their new home. They will have to unpack all their stuff and figure out what they're taking up 10 days afterward and see some friends so I will follow their lead. It's a whole lot after a solid year of art school in a different country and with 2 dads now 8,000 miles apart. I want to give them time to be and to rest."

"I have 2 very wild work weeks coming up. This is the busiest time of the semester. So just know that I'm wildly overextended starting Monday for several wild weeks!"

"But Armand wants to do a 3way with us. I showed him yr picture. I'm all for it. His days off are Tue and Wed so if one of those frees up for you that may be next!"

"I'm going to see him Thursday night in NJ after I finish work."

PART

6

I gathered my thoughts: how could anyone so fucking sensitive to "pronouns" do this to me? He had delivered a claw-hammer blow straight to my head! He didn't even wrap a towel around the hammer head to blunt evidence of the impact, like any common, self-respecting murderer would do. The only way I could see Stephen was to run off to Jesus-fuck Princeton, New Jersey, to have a "3way" with some dude I'd never even met. Like too many other people in love, all I could think of was—how the hell did I ever get into this shit? And—

And, of course (chicken as I was): How (the fuck) could I ever survive it?

I wanted the Good Fairy Godmother to come down and bestow on me some excellent tidbit of Sage Advice:

"Don't worry, Dear. Everything will work out well for you. I have this all-powerful glass slipper. I know you're a teeny-bit too old to wear it, but—"

Ye old glass slipper. There it was.

I would offer *myself* to him . . . to be as useful as possible! I had to crawl back onto that life raft, even if it were now oozing filthy Gowanus Canal water, sinking second by second. I knew, goddamn it, I had to hoist myself back on.

"I'll make time for you, Stephen," I texted. "I didn't realize what's going on—I can be flexible. I can even spend time in Princeton—for you! How's that?"

I went on—

"I have a feeling that Jody will want to be with people his own age. I can introduce him to several gay kids I know in their teens whom I met through the LGBTQ Center here. We could go to the Paradox, a bar in the East Village that has a really young crowd. It has outdoor seating, so he won't be carded if we go there."

He texted back: "They're on the phone now. lol."

"Well, tell them hello from their new gay uncle, and that we will plan some things together."

Later that evening, I went to the Metropolitan Opera with Keith to see a new production of *Lucia di Lammermor* by Donizetti, taken from one of the famous, extremely romantic "Waverly novels" by Sir Walter Scott.

I texted Stephen: "It's set in Scotland, so I'll think about you, my Scottish Lord."

He wrote back: "Keep me posted about the kilts sir! LOL"

"I will. But none of them will be nearly as interesting as the one you wore Easter."

"Yes. I'm sure that must be one of the most fab moments the Byron Gardens ever experienced."

It turned out that this production was not set in Ye Olde Scotland, but in the broken-and-busted Rustbelt Midwest of the present. "Alas, no kilts."

"Well," he wrote: "I AM from Chicago."

"I wish you were here," I wrote. "There are lots of dads with their kids. I can imagine you and Jody here."

I was surprised when he texted me back:

"Jody used to go on their own. They even bought their own opera tickets. I think they felt bad about the cost. They are a really great kid."

I thought about this: *if* Jody liked opera . . . ?

Now I realized I was in the *reverse* position of Vladimir Nabokov's little-girl-crazy Humbert Humbert. I was going *through* Lolita to get to *her* dad. I texted him:

"They can come with me to the Met. Either the Opera or the Museum. Hope you are OK. I am going to miss seeing you tomorrow. I hope you enjoy the rally on Staten Island."

I decided to call him, but all I got was voice mail.

He texted me back:

"Thx for the call. I am out of the pool eating lunch rushing to pick up Alicia so we can go out to the rally."

"Don't rush. Give me a call if you have a moment."

Later that evening, he texted me again:

"Hi I lost my voice but can text. Too much shouting and noiz. Amazing day. Turns out Alicia is besties with Michael Strong [organizer of the union rally against Amazon]. We went to my fav gay owned central NJ restaurant afterward. Magic. But I am tired."

I was extremely relieved. Like anyone else in this desperate position of dumb-ass love, I hadn't even expected to hear from him again. But during the day I felt that kind of stomach-heaving/falling-straight-down-an-elevator-shaft reaction you get when you're stuck hard on someone and he's not there after you (OK, stupidly) expected him to be.

That trap-door has suddenly opened, and whoosh—you've gone directly through it straight down to the bottom.

I'd like to say it's a difficult feeling to describe. It really isn't. It's a first cousin to nausea. You lose your appetite for everything except seeing him again. Maybe it was just the wild rush of him, like him cumming in my mouth, a need that had to be frequently repeated to be satisfied. I felt an urgency I had not felt in years, that these next several weeks would be too heartbreaking and impossible for me. Like this black curtain of time was descending right down on me, unless . . .

Oh. Jesus . . .

Unless I saw him.

Jody arrived. Stephen texted me:

"Crazy. They're here. A wild week. Lots interviews with new students. Gotta tell you. I can't actually see you till July when work slows. The 3-way with Armand—don't know if that will work. And Jody, and classes. Let's see what happens."

This was too crazy. I couldn't take another claw-hammer body blow like that. *July!* First three weeks, and then—we were still in April—he was talking close to three *full* months away. I thought: How could Stephen Hong-Moore be so cruel? How could anyone who was so fuckin' p.c.—so sensitive to every nuance of political injustice—who had told me, "I love you, too." . . . *hurt* me so badly? And how had I ended up in this strange trap, that I'd not even *set* for myself?

He'd set it. I knew it. In the most cruel, most unthinking way, he had really set it.

I know. We often do set our own traps. But let me affirm to you, as innocent and honest as God is there—*I had not set this one.* I had been through minor variations of this before. I admit it; we all have. But Stephen was so damn "cocksure" he made that antique term look modest. I kept wondering: how did this displacement happen? How did I lose so *much* of myself in this incredibly stupid guy?

It was real *Of Human Bondage*, the story of a young doctor with a clubfoot who falls in love with a vacuous, mean-spirited waitress. Somerset Maugham must have been looking down with some smirk on his face.

When I was much younger I used to think that gay men in love did what tiny one-cell paramecium did: we traded mitochondria (that energy-producing bunch of material within the nucleus of the cell) with one another. The little one-cells did it to jack up their energy—you could imagine them skipping out at night with one another and saying, "Now, buddy, let's do some mitochondria trading!" The trade with queers happened subconsciously. How else could I explain something I found no words for at the time—that peculiar, intimate giving of so much of yourself to another man, when it was so forbidden by the rest of our locker-room jock, cookie-cutter society?

Now I realized I had offered it to Stephen—this very deepest part of myself, and, *fuck-shit-piss*, my offering was impossibly devalued.

PART

7

For my own sanity, I had to end this. I couldn't take any more drowning in that wet fog with Stephen's own brain-dead undertow swirling under it. Suddenly, I could see the undertow itself—with tall Jody whom I'd never met in it; and Armand from New Jersey and his 3-some; and Stephen's college, and a lot more I didn't even know about, thrashing dangerously about with Stephen inside it.

I felt so, so stupid. And alone. And man-handled, and everything other thing you feel struggling with being in love.

I texted him: "I hope you have a good summer, Stephen."

"Me2 ready for less work after July."

I closed my eyes, then reopened them.

This whole idea seemed so nuts to me. Yes, he had no idea at all what I had been feeling . . . he who had so aggressively initiated it.

Why, I wondered, did he do this? There was no way on earth I could have seen this happening. I felt truly, thoroughly sick inside.

I texted him:

"I won't be joining you."

"I won't be joining *you*."

I had to get off this insane, dizzy, circus of a merry-go-round, before I threw my guts up.

That was the last connection we had; I didn't hear another word from him. My first feeling was I was simply no longer usable, at that moment or any moment, to him. I began to understand why people my age stop feeling these things: your feelings, once they are exposed like this, run so much deeper and more painfully. I had heard about that new expression "ghosting," when people break off without any kind of farewell or explanation.

Stephen had *ghosted* me definitely—or had I, in fact, ghosted him, with those five simple words "I won't be joining you"?

One word kept coming to me: *Entitlement*. Obviously, Dr. Hong-Moore, head of his department, was sure he was entitled to do what he had done, and now, without a doubt, this creep with the shellac mask was truly *entitled* to end it.

Ah . . . love, a more brutal sport than bare-knuckle boxing.

I kept fantasizing he would get back to me. He'd say he'd regretted what he had put me through, his callousness, his lack of regard for me.

Then I understood what was going on: I was only negotiating with something that was *not* going to happen: A fantasy. A desire. A wish. We all did that. It's where myth came from, negotiating with your desire for God's love; or eternal life; or hope against all kinds of harsh realities, until—if you're really *lucky*—reality itself does turn to your favor, or you internalize happiness so much that *that* alone does the trick. You want to believe in heaven—that somebody's going to offer it to you.

You want to *believe* in your own love returned, and the triumph of what you feel is your own special goodness?

In that case, it's just another matter of believing, your standing up against life's wicked realities—which, for the most part, are stacked against you. Generations of gypsies have made good money off this— but, hey, everyone's gotta make a living.

Still, some people do buy the perfect lottery ticket and it happens. Or fickle Cupid smiles at them and they arrive at their own perfect version of heaven. But for millions, it just doesn't happen.

But that was what I wanted. That was what this negotiation was about: *negotiating* with a fantasy, wishing to get inside those hard boundaries that I began to see were drawn strictly in Stephen's favor. I remembered that moment of getting into his purple Nissan with the bag of bubble tea and smiling and thinking that I just had to *excavate* this guy's feelings, like some archeologist going after a treasure buried for centuries. Later, I realized the opposite would happen—I would learn more about myself, stuck in this web I'd permitted myself to fall into, than I'd ever learn about him.

Finally reality did return. Slowly.

I stopped obsessing about Stephen Hong-Moore, stopped feeling alternately hurt and angry. Keith and I went back to the Opera, this time to hear *Madam Butterfly*. I had not seen the opera in years, and now I was swept up into it. "Butterfly," or Cio-Cio-san, is a beautiful young dancer who meets a handsome American naval lieutenant, Pinkerton, who basically uses her sexually, although he does have, let's say, "feelings" for her. Pinkerton has rented a house on a hilltop overlooking the bay of Nagasaki; he wants to "marry" a Japanese girl who, basically, will "come with the house." Shortly after, he plans to leave her and go back to America and marry an American woman in a "real" marriage. Japan has just opened itself up to trade with America, an American consulate is involved, along with a marriage broker, and Suzuki, Cio-Cio-san's maid. Pinkerton does marry Butterfly, in a hasty barely serious ceremony, and soon after sails back to America.

Giacomo Puccini gives us some of the most gorgeous love music in opera—and by the end, three years later, when Pinkerton returns with his American wife, and an impoverished Cio-Cio-san has been persuaded to give up the child, a blue-eyed boy she had with Pinkerton, and commits suicide, all I could feel was how close this felt to me, or to anyone whose feelings have been, say, "bludgeoned and ransacked" in love. How dangerous that fog is—and how silly is that life raft you're on!

At the end of the third act, Pinkerton shouts in vain, *"Butterfly! Butterfly! Butterfly!"*

But she's dead. And the curtain falls.

Puccini was overwhelmed with this story of female innocence destroyed by male sexual vanity, taken from a one-act play by David Belasco. The play had premiered in New York (where the Belasco Theatre still stands on Broadway) in 1900, then it moved on to London where Puccini saw it. He begged Belasco for the rights to turn it into an opera. As I left the Met's auditorium, I was overwhelmed with the story, just as Puccini must have been. I was brought back to the situation with Stephen Hong-Moore—bland Stephen's Scottish-Midwestern attraction to "other cultures," especially the "exotic" East, China, Taiwan; attractive Larry Hong.

Or, me?

Maybe it was just my "sexual energy": that of a writer who knows himself. It would not be that difficult to understand that someone like Stephen, basically emotionally blocked ("constipated"), would find a Southern-Jewish writer living in New York an excellent underground passageway to some of his own half-buried, or even long dead feelings. Just as Pinkerton did love Cio-Cio-san, but not *enough* to actually marry her . . . I'd been placed in a similar situation. Now I had to scoop up all the emotional shit left over—

—and, yep, flush it down the toilet. Thank God, time is cathartic.

It does find a place eventually to put everything. Even Stephen Hong-Moore. Certainly, for the sake of my numb brain: the modern-day equivalent of the handsome, scheming Lt. Pinkerton himself.

Like Pinkerton, Hong-Moore is the consummate user—going through people, cataloging them according to their use. Eduardo, best anal sex ever! Armand, best first date ever! Perry . . . what the hell was I? Whatever it was, it was no longer of any use to Stephen, who was—maybe simply a lesson for me. One of those life lessons that living throws at you. I had survived it, unlike poor Butterfly. Sometimes being older is good—think about all the poor Butterflies in the world. But what would opera be without them?

8

Thinking about that, I became curious about adult autism—there had to be some kind of clue inside that strange box. I wondered how many Stephen Hong-Moores were out there, especially in our very mechanized, techno-crazy world, where even vaguely normal human interactions were becoming white-tiger rare.

I decided to get in contact with Larry Hong in Taiwan. He and I were Facebook friends, so I Messengered him. I told him that I had been in touch with Stephen since their break up, and Stephen's moving to Riverdale. I knew I was being coy, like Cio-Cio-san herself: "I'm sorry [I wrote] that you are no longer here, but I hope we can stay in touch. Perhaps you can tell me more about Stephen and his autism. I know very little about it."

[I did feel like Cio-Cio-San, hiding coyly behind her hand fan—but don't we all have to use a fan occasionally?]

He sent me a very long message. Obviously, he also needed to talk about Stephen. Their relationship, why he had left the country. Racism in the U.S. was only *part* of his move. Taiwan had always felt like his home, he had many friends there, the cost of living was lower, and he could become part of the country's universal health care safety net. But, regarding Stephen: "As people we really were not on the same page." As he went on, raising their child together only made that more evident.

"A big component of the autistic brain workings is the need for structure and routine. He has a real difficulty adjusting quickly. He doesn't understand how his own actions affect other people."

[I could attest to that.]

"I had to be the 'normal' go-between between Stephen and Jody when they had conflicts and then I had to attempt to solve their problems. It did not leave me a lot of room for myself. By the end of our relationship, I was genuinely exhausted, as well as resentful and angry. To get past that I had to spend a lot of time on my own." He went on to say that the three of them were actually getting along better now. "The strange thing" was that he had to let go of Stephen "in order to actually love him again."

"The strange thing . . . ."

I thought about those words—that he had to let go of Stephen in order to love him again. God, what a mess it must have been living with him. Suddenly I had a glimmer of understanding just how I had got so mired up with Stephen, his kissing me in the car, with the softest lips, his dropping the bagels and grabbing me in the apartment. That veil, that hard shellac mask—suddenly stripped off . . . and I (or you) enter the sacred grove where men go to make love secretly and soul-baringly intimately. That mask I saw him put on in class, and then drop—it was all part of his own operating system. He could put it on and take it off at will. I, too, could not help loving him and hating him at the same time; Larry had to leave. He had to come out of it in order to end his relationship with Stephen; and then, in Larry's own way, *find* him again.

I decided at that point to let Larry know what had gone on between Stephen and me. I began with, "After he moved to Riverdale, I invited him to have dinner with me and Keith, my husband . . . . " Just telling the story was difficult—how I had been swept up in this tide of my own feelings with him, quickly submitting everything to him—

"Dear Perry," he wrote. "I'm sorry to learn about your experience with Stephen. I know the pain and anger you experienced. I need to explain to you what I know about autism. It may answer some of your questions, but I know it's not going to alleviate the pain you've been in. People with autism have extreme problems with empathy. They have a big difficulty understanding, even predicting, how their behavior impacts on other people. Because they are like this, autistic people are often labeled 'self-centered,' or 'manipulative' by people on the outside, that is people not familiar with the patterns of autism but who are affected by it."

["Manipulative." Yeah, that word did come to me, especially along with "entitled."]

Larry went on:

"I'm pretty sure that Stephen saw you as a 'friend with benefits.' He's very good at compartmentalizing sex and love. When Stephen said that he liked, or even loves you, he still does not cross the territory of friend into the territory of lover. To him, everything, and everyone, has to fit into a 'schema' so that he can operate with them according to his own limitations. I bet he had no idea that you had 'fallen in love' with him, so it was not at all necessary for him to treat you as someone important to him, that is, as a 'lover.'

"Another problem with Stephen as well as other people with autism is that they are so directed by work and the tasks and projects in front of them—you know, things they find interesting or focused on—that everybody else becomes immediately secondary."

He explained that he knew this firsthand, feeling very neglected and hurt. But Stephen could never understand this direct impact on Larry.

"If I told him how hurt I was, he would become defensive and force me to see how busy he was. He would say, 'I'm not doing this on purpose.' So everything had to be on his schedule, without taking into account any feelings of my own. I was really worn out by being put into this quandary so often. I had to not only deal with my feelings, but also handle the situations between him and Jody. I know Stephen has some very good traits, but it took a lot of energy for me to be a partner both with him and his autism."

Reading this, I started to breathe better. I wrote Larry back:

"Thank you for explaining so much to me, Larry. After I was swept up into Stephen's own intense wake toward me, and the aftermath of it, I wondered how you were able to stay with him so long. At least now I can sleep better without thinking about him. For several nights, I was kept up by this, going over and over too many times in my head what had happened between us. I felt like I was on trial, and I had really lost. I should have been smarter, more capable of acting in an adult way.

"This has really been hell for me, and I'm glad you were able to sort things out, Larry. I started to feel that I never wanted to fall in love again—who would want to be in that helpless state of begging some man to love him? That was how I felt. I hated it. Part of it must be age. Teenagers go through this, but I guess they're more resilient. At least I hope they are. But it's not always true; that's why being young is so dangerous."

Larry wrote me back that he understood what I was saying:

"Stephen is extremely intense. It's another aspect of his autism that he doesn't regulate his intensity. The truth is, he and I continued to have sex until about six months before we broke up, but sexually I never really felt connected with him—it was always about this super intensity of his that had nothing to do with how I felt inside. Anyone could have been there in bed with him; I never felt connected with him sexually, in an authentic way that was related to me. He has this problem that he can't 'read' anyone else's sexual feelings. Like they are all manikins in windows. Some manikins turn him on more than others. Most of the time he's turned on by his own feelings. *He gets excited because he's excited.*

"At first, I was really fooled. I thought all this was about me, then after a number of years I realized that it wasn't."

"What do you think it was," I wrote, "that kept you two together?"

"We had a lot of values in common. He's a good man really. He has good intentions. He's crazy about his work—finally, I realized I was simply an adjunct of it. Everything went kind of smoothly because I worked so hard to keep it going, until I just couldn't do it anymore. Jody was a big part of it. I needed Stephen's help to raise him, and when Jody became more independent, I realized I no longer had to be in this difficult situation."

I thought about what Stephen had said to me.

"He told me he could have spent the rest of his life with you; he would have just made it work."

"It was working for him. Everything fit into that 'schema' he needed. It's difficult for me to think about this from the distance we have between us, Perry. Sometimes, I admit, I get sick thinking about it."—I was reminded of my own feelings of falling down the elevator shaft—"I really want to have good thoughts about Stephen. We raised Jody together, and Jody means so much to me. He is my son, biologically and emotionally, and even spiritually. It's so amazing that I would have a son like him, who's such a part of me. Think about how many fathers never have that, or they have it in very small portions. Like their idea of a real day together is going out to a baseball game. Can you believe that? Stephen and I never had that with Jody. He wanted to be the son of two gay dads. It must have been biologically or genetically imprinted in him. It was so thrilling to us that we didn't mind making every kind of sacrifice for him. He was really the center of our life together, and then by the time he was ready to go off to school on his own, I knew that I could now go off on my own, too.

"I've found somebody else. I now have someone in Taiwan whom I feel really connected to, that his energy, sexual and otherwise, is with me. I feel like I'm another person, and I'm very happy about it. I have not been this happy since Jody was very little, and the three of us were so happy together."

Strangely enough, shortly after I got in touch with Larry, I heard from Daniel Streep. He had been thinking about me in Costa Rica and wondered how I was doing. Daniel had always been very much a free spirit; after our time in New York in gay liberation politics, he went off to live in Europe with a lover he had met in New York, a gorgeous Latino man who would later, unfortunately, die of HIV complications. The two of them easily got accepted into "Dance Now!" a very "modern" modern dance company that was more theater than dance. Daniel would easily admit that he did not have a lot of dance training and technique, but he'd been very athletic as a kid, and his body quickly adapted to the rigor of learning how to dance comparatively late in life for a dancer. José, his boyfriend, did have some dance training, and the two of them lived in Europe for a number of years, augmented by Daniel's family money.

Everything fell apart though with HIV, and Daniel took care of José until his death. After that, he felt that he really had to get away—from his life with José, Europe, dance—and he'd heard about Costa Rica, that a lot of gay Americans had started lives there. He taught English and was able to buy property. To be frank, I thought it was strange that Daniel got in touch with me when he did.

I decided that the best thing to do was play things as cool as possible, so I emailed him:

"Thank you, Daniel, for getting in touch with me. I've just been wondering if you've been in touch with Stephen Hong-Moore since his divorce from Larry. You were how I met the two of them several years ago, and I know you've been friends with them for a long time."

Daniel, who'd always presented to people this kind of "lighter than air" persona, rejecting any kind of deeper emotional attachment as characteristically ingrained with "possessiveness," which he mortally hated (it was in his mind the root of all evil), dove straight into the situation like some kind of lightning quick, self-propelled trajectile.

He sent Stephen this email, and CC'd me on it.

"Hi, Stephen. Just heard from Perry. He's wondering since you are both so close to each other in NYC, why you don't have any more of a connection? I hope I have that right!"

Muy rápido, Daniel got back to me.

"Hi Perry,

"Stephen preferred responding to me only. He's now involved with a single guy, preferring that to a balancing act of you, and a bf. I would encourage you to take big generous breaths from the Universe and thrive with the splendid mutual consensual options the Universe provides. You need, my friend, to appreciate the healthy lust and love of others, even if you, or we, can't directly participate. I believe with all my heart that letting go and forgiving are easier, more beneficial, and less stressful than holding on. The cool part is that loving friendships continue long term and present us with much wider potential for long-term personal growth. I hope this helps!"

All right. Let's get this straight—even I was a bit surprised. I had not *actually* expected Daniel to take this much of an airhead-goofy "human potential" view of life. I hadn't, but . . . knowing him as I did, even from some distances of time and location—I damn well *should* have.

My problem was, I was just not going to take any "generous breaths from the Universe." I felt like Mia Farrow in *Rosemary's Baby*. Like I, too, had landed unexpectedly into this evil shit-show of smiley wicked people comfortable with manipulation in their own sordid way.

I fired back:

"I think it's going to take more than generous breaths with Stephen Hong-Moore. I think he's a very toxic person. What I did not understand when I got swept up into this undertow with him was how much his autism would affect me, as it did everyone involved with him. I didn't understand anything about dealing with autistic people, especially autistic adults. I now know a little—and I can say they are extremely complicated people to deal with and have a relationship with. How Larry did it for so long amazes me, but raising Jody was very important to him, and that is what kept Larry in it."

Daniel answered me:

"Although I've known them for decades, I was never inclined to be as intimately engaged as you seem to have been. Have you ever heard of Katie Byron? Her 'work' may be helpful to you. She's all about turning away from your old thoughts and replacing them with new, more positive ones. Your latest email makes me think that you might appreciate considering her 'turn around' ideas. For Stephen too, it could be helpful. He has informed me that he really doesn't have the time or room for your 'drama,' Perry. I think he's a very good man, but some people are like that. We just have to get used to it.

"Hugs, Perry, and hope this, or whatever you try, helps."

9

I sent a fairly pro-forma reply back to Daniel, thanking him for his help. He didn't help. I felt fairly stupid, like you do when you've been robbed of something valuable because you forgot to close the door—or the windows. It occurred to me that I should have locked the door and the windows to Stephen when he came on to me the way he did; I should have told him that I was starting to feel . . . well, vulnerable toward him. It is the world's oldest story—if someone takes your heart away and is not worthy of keeping it, you do want to get it back any way you can.

I kept wondering why this had happened to me—what was it about me that drew him to me and then made me react the way I did?

I felt like I had to share it with someone, had to talk about it. I met my friend Philip Anthony, another writer, at the Museum of Modern Art. Philip was living in Los Angeles and we had been friends for decades. We had a late lunch at the restaurant on the second floor—it had emptied out and the two of us were fairly alone. First, I had to ask him some blunt questions.

"Do you still have sex? I mean, do you still fall in love?"

"Sure. I still have sex. I still fall in love. Why are you asking?"

"I was hoping you were past all that. I wish I was."

Then I told him the story of Stephen and me, and asked again: "Why do you think I'm like this?"

He had read a memoir I wrote about my early life. It talked about my often violent, abusive, lesbian mother and my extremely difficult, combative relationship with her.

"It was your mother," he said. "You never had any real love from her. That was obvious from your book. It was sad. I feel sorry for you—but you need to have that love, so you keep looking for it. Believe me, it's a pit a lot of us are in. I'm not totally out of it. I think no one is until you die, no matter how much bullshit they try to give us."

I was genuinely glad and touched Phillip had told me that. I felt a lot better. Writers are such great therapists really. After all, isn't that what we really deal with—life itself, seen as real?

I was almost through with this strange chapter in my life. I had stopped thinking about Stephen, although now and then I did wonder, *maybe I had just done it all wrong*—I should have simply walked away from him, and then let him come back to me at his own pace. But I knew that was complete crap; I had really fallen down into this pit of feelings, and, despite any amount of rationalism I had, knew Stephen had pushed me into it.

Just pushed me.

I sometimes wondered late at night, how many people like Stephen, with his autism, with their own special "neurodivergent" personalities, were around? I had several friends who informed me that they had OCD, Obsessive Compulsive Disorder; and I'd heard about ADHD (Attention Deficit Hyper Activity Disorder), and Dyslexia, of course, which makes reading and learning hell, and Dyspraxia, a bigger category—things that other people find normal, like being able to dress yourself or walk, you find extremely difficult. Maybe I had this with driving. I've had few comfortable moments driving, although I've been told writers as a group make bad drivers: we're always someplace else besides the road. But I wondered: if we let all these odd-performing neuro-cats out of the bag, how does that affect what we used to call "normal" personal relations?

I felt lost even in trying to figure this one out. Finally, I asked Keith. As a doctor he must have met a number of neurodivergent people, right?

"Oh, yes," he answered. "I have met a lot of them. And despite their diagnoses, I can just say one thing."

"What's that?"

"The diagnosis does not keep them from being perfect sons-of-bitches. At some point they really do have to make some room for other people, we 'neurotypicals' you could say. It's hard for us to deal with them, and for them to deal with us, but at some point, they can really destroy your life; I learned that over time."

We were in the car, driving back from shopping when he said that. He was driving, and, like I said, driving is horrible for me. It really did put things strangely into their rightful place, kind of like being shaken out of a nightmare, and then falling back to sleep again. I had spent a number of nights tossing around about this, feeling like I said, on trial. Now I realized I could go back to sleep and wake up once more just as myself.

the end

The Seduction of Perry

There is a time in early November when Chicago seems like an unsettling small town rather than a big city. The big Chicago cold hasn't blasted in yet, but the air has a tremor, a definite threat to it, and even though the winter wind has hardly begun you're aware it may be waiting around the corner and, if you are not ready, kick you hard in the guts. The natives with their red Midwestern faces still jog along the lakefront and nice-looking kids in shorts and high school sweaters amble along behind the joggers, acting as if fall has not yet abandoned them. It's possible to detect a distant tingle of Christmas coming up, and still feel wonderful about being there. I go to Chicago enough on business and have seen the city, as it emerges out of the flat plains, be numbing, mean, and cold. But other times, when I arrived in spring or the crispness of autumn, it had a freshness and ease that Eastern cities didn't. Two years ago, I was there in November for a book sales conference, glad that the blunt force of winter hadn't yet set in.

The conference was held at the Hennison, an old hotel in the Loop with ancient creaky elevators that felt like they dated back to the Fire. I was staying in a small, eighteenth-floor room at the top; it took me forever to get up there. I arrived early on a Friday evening, and the next day I would have to pitch my line of spring season books in front of about fifty sales reps for my distributor. I work for a small press that publishes gay books, and after years in the business know that the rhythm of sales conferences and pitching your next list can get into your blood. On one hand it is frightening, and you feel like a fifth grader giving your report on the Indians in front of the class. You gotta make sure: Fly zipped? Socks match?

On the other, you can feel like Marco Polo, bringing something fabulous back from the East, then unrolling it to the amazement of the jaded Borgia court. Certain books can do that, and even the most jaded reps will perk up and say, "Wow! Never thought of that, maybe this one'll do it!"

When that happens, a charge of electricity runs through the air and there is that moment of recognition which lovers have when they encounter each other for the first time. Even after twenty years, I still feel there is something mysterious and disarming about working in books. Each story in itself has a hidden story, the unseen one of its origins: where it came from, how it came to be public, and, of course, who will believe it enough to want to possess it—buy it?

That Friday evening I met three sales reps and two other publishers in the Hennison lobby. We talked for a while, then settled into the small hotel bar—muted TV, football—with a beer. Mostly the usual talk: what we expected that spring at the book shows, in the stores, on the road with our authors. It was in the 1990s and there was still an old-fashioned, low-glow glamour to our business, involving numbers of bright people, their connections and desires. Books don't have that all-or-nothing, high-pressure glitziness of the movies, or later what would be found in technology. As we say, books are read one at a time and sold one at a time. They're still private and intimate. Most of us in the business remember that delicious rite of childhood, reading "dirty" books by flashlight. The books you kept under your bed, the adventure books or sex books, or any book that said something special to you that no one else could. Books with a keyhole in them: Opening up new rooms in your own heart and soul.

Rooms that you were often extremely fearful about entering.

In turn, book people themselves had a way of spilling their guts out to you that could be quite disarming; but you took this in stride, mostly because you don't want the business to become such a cutthroat affair that it never happened. We fall in love with certain books. They come our way and we want to devour them, tell the whole world about them; we become obsessive about them. You might try to hide this and talk about the nuts-and-bolts of the business, but there was always the question of how did this bit of sublime magic come into your life, and why did it leave you so disarmed, feeling suddenly so unaccountably vulnerable, yet aware of a unique experience that had just been revealed to you?

We were starting to get that way at the Hennison bar, talking about books that never made it, that sold only a few thousand copies—sometimes even only a few hundred—when we wanted them to swan dive onto the bestseller lists. We wanted them to open up into the popular culture like roses in full bloom on a busy street, so that anyone could sniff them. And we wanted masses and masses of other people to open themselves up to them, too, just the way we did.

In short, we wanted miracles that unfortunately didn't happen. Like love sometimes, they just didn't take.

We sat at the bar long enough, then afterwards went out to an Italian restaurant for dinner. I was starting to get talked out; like I said, book people have a way of spilling their guts out to you and Randy Guller, a sales rep from Baltimore, and I, off to ourselves, had this conversation that became, well, I admit it—it became too quickly, too embarrassingly . . . intimate.

It started out about my books. "I'm not gay," he said, "but there's something about your books I like selling. I go into a store, and the managers have this funny look on their faces. It's, you know, like, 'Gay books? What do I do with gay books?' Then I show them yours and I tell them that—anyway, I tell them that I've looked into them. 'They're all right,' I say. 'Your customers will *really* like them.' "

He smiled at me and we gazed at each other, and suddenly I felt like we were talking about more than books. Of course, because of my very queer press, I didn't have to "come out" as gay to him. He knew my story, and maybe it was just from too much alcohol and book talk and being in Chicago before the weather turned bad, but I felt him getting—OK—physically closer to me.

Then realized I wasn't simply imagining it.

"I'm getting married," he revealed, slightly above a whisper. "For the first time." I congratulated him. He shrugged his beefy shoulders; I could tell that he was well built, even under his winter tweed sports jacket and tie. Evelyn, his fiancé, was six years older than he was. "She's been married before. She has two kids, see?"

Other conversations at the table swirled loudly around us, as I leaned slightly toward him.

"I can see that could be difficult," I said, and licked some wine off my lips.

He looked scared, thirty-four, never married; the whole idea of "going over to the woman's side," as he put it, jarred him. "She wants to live out in the suburbs, so her kids can have nice schools. God, those dreary Baltimore suburbs!" I nodded my head. "Perry, it was nice when I visited her and the kids. But now I'll live with them. What d'you think?"

Our eyes connected; his pupils opened up to me and I felt for that split second like I was being sucked into his very soul. I hesitated, then said: "You have to keep some life of your own."

I said that without moving my eyes from him. That was my advice, nothing else. It was not a come-on, although, in some corners, it could have been construed that way. He had a young, charming, attractive face, with the kind of attentive lips and nose you might find on a life-guard. His dark glossy hair was starting to thin a bit on top; lines near his eyes said he was thoughtful.

Suddenly he looked at me in a way that confirmed heterosexual men rarely allow themselves to do: Soft, touching, deeply vulnerable.

"A life of my own?" He shrugged. "You're right. But . . . how do you do that, when you're married?"

"Difficult," I said, becoming aware that the restaurant was getting warmer. Maybe it was a third glass of not-bad chianti, or the warmth that books themselves spread over people. Before, we had been talking about books, breathing them in, that rich, old-fashioned, papery full-ness of books; of books that mean more to you than simply paper. Im-pulsively, I really wanted to lean over more, and . . . now I can admit it—kiss him.

What an impulse! I had to remind myself that the evening was still about business, and I was not going to let a seductive, though "open-ly" hetero sales rep push me into something that later I might regret. Things were getting a little too close. So after dinner, when Randy and the others were all heading for another bar that had a jazz combo, I ex-cused myself and went back to the hotel. Up the elevator with the slow cables turning, to the eighteenth floor, to my small room with the steam steadily hissing.

2

When you've stayed in enough of them, hotel rooms
possess an unsettling finality, something that hotel lobby whores have
known how to use for ages: to put it in a nutshell, these cubicles with
their little refrigerators stocked with expensive snacks are hopelessly
lonely. I thought about Randy Guller with a distinctly regretful pang.
Maybe something *could* have happened. Who knew what oddly-slanted
game of seduction was going on? Was he calling out for help, just before
going down the aisle; or merely twirling me around his attractive bache-
lor fingers? Was he reaching out to me as just another "regular guy" who
only *happened* to be queer, or was he putting himself in a very irregular
situation?

I thought about it as I brushed the Italian food out of my teeth.
Then said: why put yourself into a bag you can't get out of? Chicago
(and my part of the book world) was only so big. I'd have to see Randy
the next day, and then at the next sales conference I'd have to pitch another season of books to him. He was a part of the cycle, simple as that.

I needed a good night's rest, and I did sleep well. But waking up
early and seeing a gray Midwestern November light drifting through
my narrow turret-like window, I realized how alone I was. The steam
started up again.

That day was hard, but not as bad as I'd thought it would be. At ten
I was given thirty minutes to present twelve books, which comes out to
less than three minutes a book—about par for a hectic sales conference.
The reps had been there since eight, and some, like Randy, had been
out the night before. I could see that "let's-get-on-with-it" look on their
faces. Not that fast of a talker, with only four more minutes left, I still
had three more books to cover. The reps started gazing at their watches,
swallowing coffee, and I began to speed through. Randy, who looked
hung over, winked at me; the other reps started to smile, and our conference manager, Joshua, looked up.

"Take eight more minutes, Perry," he suggested.

I pretended to mop my brow, then finished and thanked them.
Somewhere out in the world there were several oblivious but happy

authors who would not have to hear me racing through their beloved masterpieces. I sat in the lobby afterwards, then had an overpriced lunch in the hotel with Rachel Schlesinger, the New York rep, and Barry Middleton, a corpulent rep from Ontario.

"We are starting to do exceedingly well with our *homo-seks-ual* market," Barry said, stretching the word out. "But," he cleared his throat— "Can you tell me anything more about this new book you are doing. The one for—how do you say?—'leather fetishists?'"

Rachel shot me a knowing look, and I went back into my pitch, wondering perhaps if I were giving out more information than Barry, in his gray tweed vest, could handle. Afterwards, I left the Hennison and met with a Barnes and Noble manager, and then with Wilbert, a buyer from Borders who had been nice to me in the past. This time Wilbert was in a "why bother me?" mood, which bothered *me*, but it was over with quickly enough. I decided to walk around the Loop a bit. It was only three thirty, but it felt like twilight already, with that watery cool light that filtered in in November, perhaps from the icy water off Lake Michigan.

I went to Marshal Fields, then trudged back to the hotel. Randy was talking in the lobby, and we grinned to each other like two conspirators who needed another excuse get back together for a murder. I was starting to get a tension headache, and went back up to my room.

There would be a conference cocktail party later, and I steeled myself for it, took a short nap, downed some vitamins and a Xanax, then went to it, mixing, mingling, trading business cards. Some reps broke out and told me what a good presentation I'd made—like your teacher from fifth grade complimenting you from her desk; I "gee shucks"-ed it all, shook more hands, then saw Randy in the corner of my eye off to himself. We suddenly both looked extremely guilty, like we had stretched the rules and now it was time to slink back to our respective corners. I knew this, then left.

I returned to my room, changed clothes, got into jeans and a leather jacket, and put on a pair of black boots: it was now time for me to have a good time. The doorman asked if I wanted a cab, and I decided why not? It was a splurge, but I deserved it after facing book reps and store managers, especially that ass Wilbert from Borders. The doorman whistled a cab up, and I got in. I told the Pakistani driver that I wanted to go up to North Belmont. Boys Town. About twenty dollars later, he dropped me off at the Chicago Eagle. It was still early, pre-dinner really, but I wanted to be in a different environment and this was all leather and grunting men. I had a beer, then found a small Greek restaurant in the neighborhood, and afterwards walked around a bit.

The glory of Chicago is that there are still distinct neighborhoods. Even the gay area had comfortable houses, tree-lined streets, and big leafy backyards. I strolled along killing time, then without warning it got colder and very, very dark, as if even the streetlights were now covered with burlap. The wind started sweeping in with a loud hiss and a rumbling cough that I didn't like. It reminded me of the cough of a dying man. One of my friends who had died had that cough, and now the unruly wind in Chicago possessed it.

I started to turn around. I could have gone back to the Eagle or another bar, but decided it was too chilly for that. Why not the baths? Man's Land, an old bathhouse, was a block down from the Eagle. On Saturday nights it got some of the Eagle crowd and, sometimes, if you saw someone you liked at the Eagle but did not feel right about approaching him, you'd find him far less inhibited by clothing at the baths. The attendant, a wiry kind of rodeo-cowboy-looking guy with a dark trimmed beard and tar-black eyes, took my money and let me in.

3

I got a room. For someone who doesn't make a lot of money, it was another splurge but I needed something to blow my mind out, as we used to say; or do people still say that? I found my room, got out of my clothes, then went down to the mildewed basement steam room and showered. The shower, instantly cold and needle-fine, woke me up, getting me in the mood for some excitement.

It was still early, not quite ten, but already plenty of men were walking around. I went back to my room, opened the door slightly, sat on the small cot with the light on and waited.

Nothing happened for what seemed like forever, as a parade of guys quietly passed my room. Then they notched up the sound system into a obnoxiously loud wall of pounding disco, making the men who'd been casually parading by before speed around faster, like a carousel brakes-off loaded with insane horses, and I was a three-year-old kid with no ticket to ride, standing at the side watching.

No one even nodded.

There are times at the baths when you feel like you're covered in gold dust. Men stop; smile; touch you; desire you and the magic of the evening starts deliciously. The usual cruel games slow down, as Venus hands you one of her precious apples and you pass it on to the next guy, who takes an affectionate bite from it. Then, there other times when you're sure you're covered in barnyard shit. You can't give yourself away in a bull market, not even with a hundred blue chip shares thrown in.

Of course, it's all in your head. It's the same you, right? No matter what; but who can explain it? Is it just the fickleness of faggots—or something else, a kind of aura you give off? A freaky chemistry that oozes from your heart and groin and announces: "I'm here. I have what you want. So want me!"

But they *don't.* In fact nobody does.

That evening—after about an hour and a half of this frantic merry-go-round never stopping for me—I was sure I was covered in pure crap. Guys passed me, giving me a look of such rejection that it made my stomach turn. Callous, distasteful, contemptuous—that look came from young beauties a thousand percent sure of themselves, and *alte kakers* whose confidence had abandoned them eons ago. It came from white men, black men, brown men, Asians, three fat kids who constantly dished with each other, and two angular, bony, super-emaciated specimens who looked like vultures. I expected them to levitate and start circling above my head any minute: I was definitely dead meat. They all walked past me, abrasive as that Chicago wind outside, giving me a look like I'd either been turned into a pillar of salt, or a mound of garbage.

Objectively, I can say I'm not *that* bad looking. Even slightly above average, actually. In my younger days, when I still had a lot of hair and that glow you emit then, I'd been a *looker*. It's no secret: when you're a looker, you know it. And, let me say, being realistic (and all things being exactly what they were), I still knew where I stood in the international queer meat market, knowing that there were men to whom I did appeal; often of about my age, or sometimes even younger. We were a part of that generation that still read books, remembered hand-written letters that came to you in the mail; and that felt that being young and gay, at least on *retrospect*, we could actually be nice to each other. Not always exactly smoochy, but with little effort we could certainly bestow a faint smile or two.

Then panic hit me.

Suppose the warmth and sexual closeness I yearned for was just not going to happen that night; and every man would speed past me, sneering at me? It made me yearn for Randy who had been so naked to me, really, in his own repressed way; even with all the obstacles (those "gay"-"straight" labels, and the approaching wedding) between us. I saw Randy telling me his story, bathed in kindness, panicking about his marriage, exactly as I was panicking at the baths.

I dimmed the light in my cubicle, then turned it back up slightly. Men passed, some whispering, others speaking loudly as if I didn't exist. They slowed a bit, smirked, then went on; I saw in their closed faces nothing but open contempt.

But why for me?

Finally I slammed the door in the face of the last jerk who squinted in, giving me this frigid rejecting look, a tall, beefy, corn-fed, muscular blond who held his attractiveness out to me like it were some enticing candy he would quickly slap my face for wanting.

He turned, and I slammed the door. The shit! How did I know he was a shit? Well, wasn't there a kind of queer radar that allowed you to know so much more than you were supposed to? Gaydar. O.K. I knew it. He stared, started off and I slammed the door. I could hear it hit the back of his head, then nothing. A few seconds later, I heard his footfalls (he was big, maybe a hundred and eighty pounds) clump down the hall.

Why were all these queers so cruel? It all started to add up to a very hard day, with the eerie ghosts of the wind themselves howling outside. I turned the light off and lay alone in my tiny cubicle, looking out into the darkness where I saw myself waiting, as, virtually, another ghost. Unfortunately, I didn't have another Xanax, but I could have used it. I closed my eyes and was immediately back at dinner with Randy Guller, the two of us still talking about books. Now we were seducing each other with books. Smiling, taking our clothes off. He was straight, he insisted, but he was going to let me seduce him . . . with books.

There were all these books we were going to read naked together, holding each other while we read. I started to turn the pages, and re-alized their surfaces were now formed of Randy's beautiful flesh. It was slightly dappled with the warm, golden toasty traces of his skin. I could see a surge of warm tones on his rolling prairie of a chest, with just enough dark wild hair blowing over it; his big arms, his powerful, farm-boy shoulders. There were blushes of rose and vermillion and ochre on his pale belly, deepening towards his crotch. There his sex organ waited, glowing even more, like a warm pillar of pink desert granite in the sunset.

I was reading his skin with my eyes, my fingers, even my lips, as if the words on it were not simply printed but stood up naturally slightly above it, and I could feel them with a pure, responsive sensation like warm skin itself touching mine. Occasionally, while reading (even when fully dressed), a line of print changed for me into small, glimmering lights glowing directly in front of me. Now fully naked, the magic of finely written words swam slowly over me. Suddenly I wanted to read something, just to calm myself. But I had not taken a single book with me to the baths.

I started to think about the books I had read and the people in them. Tolstoy's Anna Karenina; her misguided and inevitable love for Vronksy. Dostoyevsky's Mischkin, the "idiot," and Thomas Mann's Aschenbach, who died in Venice for a Polish boy with whom he could not even speak. Melville's Billy Budd and Forster's Maurice, and Conrad's "secret shar-er," whispering to a handsome swimmer, a psychic twin hiding in his cabin. Proust's Albertine—who was really his chauffeur named Albert (talk about every story having a story!); and Virginia Woolfe and John

Cheever, Edmund White, and Samuel Delany; and more and more books. They just rippled out at me in the dark, like so many more gorgeous examples of human seductions and couplings. Whole chapters and passages bearing exquisite pin-pricks of light around them, "illuminations" from the very soul of the writing itself, bringing to me something I distinctly longed for, this soul-restoring nurturance in the secret heart of sex.

Sentences—and sentences and more sentences—appearing like the most intimate dialogues, like being in bed with someone and hearing him say something so revealing that it rekindled your own appetite for him. But who did that anymore? Who opened his heart? Certainly it did not happen at the baths—so I started to feel better, maybe if only from realizing that it was silly to feel any worse. After all I was a stranger here; and all of my peculiar fantasies about books that I had acquired over the years, how could they have resonance at this place? Perhaps it just wasn't the right night for the magic I sought from some enchanting stranger to happen here.

Simple as that. And I'd have to look somewhere else for him.

I turned the light back on low, cautiously opened the door and peered out. The hallway was empty, and quiet. Then everything started again: The loud sound system. The empty parade. But it had slowed down a bit, then someone stopped at my door. He smiled. I mean really smiled. And I was afraid even to breathe because he was young, barely out of his early twenties. And amazingly, ravishingly attractive.

His loveliness blew over me, like a wonderful mist coming out of a lake: something Arthurian, mysterious. It carried with it the soft young smoothness of his skin, his beautiful deep chest, his wide shoulders that had a fog-milkiness to them, as if he had recently emerged from some warmer, grander version of Lake Michigan itself. His neck was—it was "poetic." As if it were another perfect example of the smooth, regular beauty of his features. This young man seemed to come from a different period, a more graceful, charming, and secretive age, like the swimmers in an Eakins painting.

My eyes swam over to his face, begging just to be allowed to *"dog-paddle"* around him. I thought about Whitman. Gerard Manley Hopkins. A. E. Housman. And I became afraid—truly *afraid*—something we become in the fleeting presence and shimmering, physical reality of beauty.

I felt frozen, but made myself nod at him, as if I had become a puppet in his hands. I held my breath and he eased into the doorway. Then I noticed, even in the dim light, that his eyes were an amber green, luminous like a white cat's, fringed with soft, sable lashes. His hair was also jet black, which made his skin appear whiter and more dazzling. His skin made me want gallons of light to be pouring in around us, bathing us; but it was not. Light was not pouring in, but he came in like gold. I sat up and motioned as if in a dream for him to come closer.

He took off his towel.

I stood up, we embraced, and I drew his soft, young mouth that tasted like fresh water to mine. Rolling my lips over his neck, I wanted to write my name there, as if I were only a bamboo pen dipped in India ink, and also might write on his chest, stomach, and hips. My lips settled on his small nipples, and he started to brush my hair, peppered with gray, with his hands raking through it. I knelt and as I took him, I had this image in my mind of sucking forth light from darkness. A light that came from its own source, released now by the sweet, ready magic of his loins.

His skin was cool, and I found this marble coolness unsettling and yet also immensely attractive. I got back up, and then we lay together on the narrow cot. He asked me my name. "Perry," I told him.

"I'm Adam," he said, his voice of medium register, not too deep or too high; still a boy's voice, hardly that of an adult. It sounded distant, shy, unsure of itself, and I knew that I wanted him to talk more, just to hear him. Answering my questions, he told me he was new in town and had only been in Chicago for a short while. I listened exactly as I had to Randy Guller, but strangely calmer, without any consciousness of games going on between us.

I wasn't sure what to say, but the soft ripple of his words soothed me, and I wanted to take each sound that he spoke and put it into my mouth like a magic potion. Instead I settled for his lips, kissing him over and over again, wanting simply to own his kisses for that moment in the baths, which should have been enough to satisfy me.

But desire itself, like a sly banker offering me yet another round of credit, started to come back in. Before I had been too frightened of this beautiful young man even to admit the degree and presence of my desire for him. I'd felt that if he had only stayed there for a moment, it would have been enough. But it was not; and now desire came stalking back in, even though Adam still felt cold, his marble-white flesh not absorbing a drop of my warmth. This made me anxious, not simply because he didn't feel for me the intensity of desire that I felt for him—that's to be expected in any situation. But suppose he got bored? Suppose he decided to get up and walk out? What would I do?

Rationally, I wouldn't have been any worse off than I was about half an hour earlier. But I would be left only with the unfulfilled fantasy of him, that vivid shine of his beauty that was now animating the very air of the tiny room. What could I do without it? Totally lost, I would have to return to the Hennison, back up in the slow elevator to my room; alone, on a top floor.

"What would you like me to do?" I asked.

He broke into a shy, dimpled smile, warming me from my toes up. If he'd said, "Let's rob a bank and kill a few people!" I would have given it a lot of consideration.

I waited as he looked at me with those amber-green eyes. "What do you want me to do?" I repeated.

He looked away, and I felt my heart pound in my ears. The pounding got worse. Then I realized that he had stopped my left ear with his tongue. His tongue, too, felt cool, chilling me thoroughly. He took my earlobe into his mouth, and softly bit it. My skin tingled. He was a young, cool *kouros*, I thought, thinking of those beautiful statues of adolescent Greek gods that I had been infatuated with as far back as I could remember.

"Adam," I said, repeating his name as he kissed my ear again. "Adam."

His tongue left my ear, then he whispered, "This is funny, but . . . would you consider leaving with me? I can't stay out late. See, I'm not allowed to."

I smiled, looking into his emerald eyes that sparkled with the liveliness of goldfish darting through the teasing forest of an aquarium. "Do you live at home with your parents?"

"Naw." He shook his head. "Just a roommate. He doesn't like me out late."

"Roommate? You mean a lover, don't you? You can be honest. Would he be angry if I came home with you? I mean, is that what you want me to do, go home with you?"

He shook his head. "Naw, Hank—that's his name—he's not a lover. I don't have a lover. Hank won't be angry. He does things for me. Takes care of me. Cooks. He probably won't even be up. You might like him, too. He's older than me. Some guys even find him attractive, in a kind of kinky way. I hope you don't think this is weird."

He smiled the same shy, dimpled smile. *Weird?* What was weird? He hadn't even mentioned the possibility of murder and cannibalism yet, and for more time with him, I definitely would have considered either, or both.

No. This was definitely not weird.

He **kissed me some more,** with his sweet penetrating kiss, and I noticed that he was starting to get slightly warmer. What could I do? I couldn't keep my hands off him. Was he suggesting a ménage with this "roommate"? Who cared? Even if the roommate were thoroughly repulsive, to question his invitation seemed impossible. Even ridiculous.

Repulsive? How could I use a word like "repulsive" about his room-mate? All the other queers at the baths had thought that about me—and why? Was there something about me that *only* this young man could see, some intensely deep facet of my nature, my yearning, hungering, need-ful self? Maybe only he could see inside me, and, at the same time, only he, this lovely young god, had seen how deeply desirable I was.

But how could something like that be true?

I didn't want to think about it.

I told him of course I would go home with him. He smiled and watched as I dressed myself.

We started downstairs to where he had his clothes in a locker, pass-ing about a dozen men, many of whom had previously been totally indifferent to me. At first I was sure I could see questions on their faces, and their morbid curiosity infuriated me, as if they were saying: "What was he doing with this gorgeous young thing?" The two of us together—the very idea must have bothered them. I saw flashes of interest in their dull faces, but I was smart enough to realize that it was merely desire for Adam. This *cool* attractive young man was what they wanted. Then I saw something else.

Fear—just a flash of it.

Then they were all gone, disappearing quickly. Perhaps they were experiencing the same fear I had, when Adam first came into my room. I even saw the beefy blond I had slammed the door on. He looked at Adam. His face froze as I smiled at him. But I was positive that this shallow creep was only disappointed that I would get to leave with this beautiful young man. I felt like I was in some kind of strange story, like

Dr. Jekyill and Mr. Hyde, except in this case it was *Dr. Jekyll and Dr. Jekyll.* I mean I was the same person I had been before, but now, of all things, I was going home with this beautiful young man.

Adam retrieved his nondescript boyish clothes from his locker. We brought our used towels to the front desk, and I picked up my wallet that I had left there for safekeeping.

It felt warmer outside than earlier. Adam told me that he lived only about seven or eight blocks away, and as we began walking I asked him if he were still in school.

"Naw. Gave up school years ago. About when I met Henry. Hank. The guy I told you about."

"Your roommate?"

"Yeah. He does things for me. It's nice having him around." He grinned self-consciously, as a naive school kid might. "He gets such a kick out of serving me. It's about the only thing he wants to do with his life. I dunno why. Anyway, who knows? Maybe you'll get t'meet him, and see."

"You're sure he won't be angry?"

"Naw," he repeated. "The truth is, he really does what I want him to do. But like in a nice way."

"What did you do in school?"

"Not much. There isn't a lot you can learn anymore. The world's too crazy. You gotta be on top of the rules. Sometimes you even have to make 'em up by yourself. Don't you think so?"

I told him it was true that the world was crazy. I worked with books, I said, in publishing. He told me that he didn't do a lot of reading, but that he wanted to. "One day when I'm not so busy." He smiled again with that lovely, ravishing smile of pure white skin, beautiful teeth, and green eyes, then added: "You'd be surprised how much work there is to do for a young man like myself."

I stopped for a moment and looked at his bright smile that seemed so unlike Randy Guller's extremely controlled face. We strolled down several blocks of homes and apartment buildings lined with big trees. Lights were still on in some windows. The lights gave their comfortable rooms a warm, yellowish glow. I started to feel colder and zipped my leather jacket up closer. He wore only a thin beige, cheap-looking windbreaker over a gray, buttoned-down oxford cloth shirt; it was all so non-descript looking that except for his handsome face there was a chance you might not really notice him.

But I would have noticed him. I knew it. On the subway, or walking out of a store, he would not have been invisible to me. Then in the middle of the next block, we were there. It was a big, solid-looking brick building, three stories, set somewhat back from the sidewalk, with two short sets of concrete stairs up to the door. There were no lights on at all. "Hank's probably asleep," Adam explained, flashing that smile again.

I nodded. Obviously, the house belonged to Hank and I was sure he had to be up early for work; that must have been the story, despite Adam's reference to being "served" by him. Henry, or Hank, was asleep, and did not want to be disturbed by his young friend returning home with company.

Adam took his key out, unlocked a big front door, and we entered a cramped, dark hallway with a coat rack then a spacious living room, furnished with what looked like more than a century old antiques. I noticed them even in the dark, as I tried to keep from bumping into heavy Victorian chairs, blocky side tables and other large pieces. He switched on a table lamp shaded with a floral amber-glass globe, and the room became immediately cheery, glowing with a gentle warmth which made me relax. I looked into Adam's eyes, at their amber luminescence that had gathered little silver daggers of light into them.

He smiled adorably.

I looked around at the pictures on the walls, large Victorian oils of knightly processions and moonlight vigils; strange, half-naked wrestling matches between gorgeous angelic male figures; and some medieval tales that, as a child, I vaguely remembered seeing in illustrated books. The pictures glowed with a jeweled intensity in the antique light surrounding them.

"They're beautiful," I said. "Are they your roommate's?"

"Mine," he said possessively. "Everything here's mine." He patted my back, and that self-conscious, school kid grin returned as he added: "Maybe even you."

He switched off the light and led me up the stairs. On the second floor we came to a door, his bedroom I guessed, and we walked in. The room was starkly empty and very cold. There was only a mattress on the floor and a small chest of drawers. "You can put your things on the floor," Adam whispered. "Wait a minute, I'm going to see if Hank's asleep."

"Hank, your roommate?"

"Sure. You can say that."

He stepped out quietly. I got undressed and then slid under the covers. It was warm and surprisingly comfortable there. We were in the back of the house. Moonlight streamed through a large single window. Sometimes it became sprinkled with leafy patterns on the hardwood floors from some nearby tall trees. Adam returned a moment later. He took off his clothes, dropping them on the floor so that it seemed as if he, too, had emerged, pale and naked, from the trembling, dancing outside light. He got under the covers and covered my mouth and face with kisses.

Then he announced: "Hank's asleep. I think we should fall asleep, too."

"Why?"

"I'm tired. Suppose I wake you up in the middle of the night, and we make love then? How's that?"

Only too wonderful, I thought. The whole scene under the covers with this beautiful young man seemed as ecstatically pure and story-like as the pictures in the living room. I pulled him into my arms, pressing my lips to the smooth white blossom of his neck, and then fell asleep.

PART
6

I have no idea how long I had been out—and don't remember a single dream. But when I awoke in darkness, the moon was gone and Adam had left with it. I was freezing and had to pee, something that happens to older men, so the first order was finding a place to take care of that. I went out into the hall, saw two doors and luckily picked one that led down another short hall to a bath. The bath seemed fairly ancient too, with a john that had a wooden tank over it and a pull chain to flush it; I hadn't seen anything like that in ages. Even if all the furnishings in the house did belong to Adam, I still wondered how old Hank must have been to have had something like this. I was still certain that the house itself must have belonged to him. I finished urinating and carefully pulled the chain. It made an awful loud groaning sound that seemed to shake the toilet. But in a house that old, everything might make a loud sound.

I wondered about Adam; had he gone in to sleep with Hank? Even if Adam were only Hank's "roommate," perhaps there was some kind of agreement between them, such as Adam would lure men back to Hank, and then they would enjoy them together. I had known this type of thing to happen with couples who had been together for a long time, often when one was older. Not that this always happened, but Adam was certainly a lure for anyone, as he had been for me.

I was eaten up with curiosity; questions rumbled through my head as loudly as the old toilet flushing. I hurried back to Adam's room, pulled on my undershorts and came back out. Now it felt even darker in the hallway, perhaps from my tightening nerves, knowing that I was doing something I shouldn't be doing. The second door was locked.

For all I knew it could have only been a closet, so I decided to try the third floor. I was fearful but curious, as cautiously I started up the dark stairs to the third floor, aware of every creak and groan my bare feet made on the old hardwood, and every sigh that the house made as it responded to the wind outside or even the passing weight of a truck on the empty streets in the dead of night. It must have been about three in the morning. What a headache, I was sure I'd end up with the next day, but at that moment the only thing I could be truly sure of was my desire for Adam. To have him again next to me with my arms around him was all I wanted; even as cool and distant as he was, a distance that I tried to explain by the years between us.

At the landing I saw only one door, several yards away from me. A faint red light spread under it, making the door's dark bottom take on a pale glow. Approaching it, I heard some very heavy, very difficult breathing like a winded runner might make attempting to catch his breath. Interrupting the breathing was a series of muffled utterances that sounded like begging.

"Le . . . le . . . le," I heard. I put my ear directly to the door: "Le' me . . . le' me."

Le' me—what? I wondered.

I compressed myself and crouched, squinting intently as I could through the door's tiny keyhole. The noise ceased and all was black darkness until my eyes became more adjusted to the dimness within. There was Adam's beautiful body. Pale, almost floating, like a silvery apparition on an old silent film, remote; ghostlike.

I stared harder with one eye, trying to see with whom he was, but all I saw from where I crouched was Adam's naked figure moving in the slowest motion.

"Please. Le' me go."

The words were so faint they seemed composed of sheer breath, as if there were no tongue involved.

"I served y' . . . I di'. . . please."

"You don't fool me," Adam whispered above the quieter pleas. "You'll go down there, Hank, and kill him!"

"You hurt me," the voice moaned, stretching every word out. "I won' har-rrm him. Please. I beg you. Pleeeeee-se!"

I strained my eyes, but I could see nothing beyond Adam. My legs, weakened from cold, the hour, and my lack of sleep, started to wobble. But my curiosity, which seemed at that moment only another side of desire itself, got the best of me. I rose, knowing I was opening myself up to anything, and with my knees cracking in the silence, I carefully tried to turn the doorknob.

The knob made a grating sound that stripped the silence from the hall, like rusty hinges to the doorway of a tomb. That noise ushered me into the room. Adam turned immediately and looked at me.

"Perry," he said softly but with absolutely no irritation in his voice. "Why did you follow me up here?"

"I'm sorry," I apologized. "I guess I missed you down there."

"Ohh," he sighed. He smiled, nodding, knowing he had me in his lovely hands. "It's just . . . well. See. Hank's been kind of bad. A little while ago while you were sleeping, he came down. He's been jealous—I told him not to be. I mean, what are you to me anyway? I tried t' explain that, but he has this ugly nature. So I've had to . . . " he hesitated, then explained: "Hold him up here."

7

I **gazed quickly around. A faint, reddish light** came from an old lamp fitted with a single small bulb like the sort customarily seen on an outdoor Christmas tree. The room had been outfitted, obviously, for purposes focusing on pleasure. Mattresses on the floor; restraints on the walls. A long folding table for massage work. But I could not see anyone else.

"Where," I asked cautiously, "Is he?"

"Over there." Adam motioned to a corner. "I put him under that blanket. It gets pretty cold here. See?"

Now I knew where the voice came from.

"Make him release me!" The voice was louder now and very hoarse, literally shredded with pain. "Make him! I'm old. I won't hurt nobody. I'm in agony! *Pleeeee-se!*"

"What are you doing?" I asked Adam, and walked over to the large shape hidden under a stiff old Army blanket. It squirmed at my feet as I crouched toward it. What was under it breathed with that dying man's unsettling rasp, that extremely strained rattling sound that I hated in the wind in Chicago. "You've got to let him out," I pleaded. "Maybe he's dying?"

The young man laughed. "Don't be a fool, Perry. Hank's has been dying for years." He walked over and kicked the shape under the blanket with the ball of his bare foot.

"You're hurtin' me!" the voice cried. "Why? I'm old. You tied me up. What can I do to you, Adam? I begged you to come live with me. I gave my life up for you. Now you tied me up and threw me over here!"

I got up and faced Adam.

"You've got to let him go," I said. "This isn't right. I'll leave if that'll help."

Adam smiled at me sweetly. "But you don't want to leave, Perry, do you? You want to stay here and make love with me, right?"

It was true; I nodded my head.

"So, the choice is yours." He looked at me, his green eyes steady, unblinking. "I wouldn't untie him before, as long as you're in the house. But if you tell me you want me to do it—sure, I will."

I drew Adam to me and tried to embrace him. He was as cold as ice, but I kissed him impulsively, while Hank moaned under the blanket, pleading, with that painful, half-strangled, horribly injured sound in every utterance. I began to weep; I'm not sure why, but I did. It was too pathetic, listening to that sound with this beautiful naked boy in my arms. "You've really got t' let him go," I whispered.

"Yes," Adam surrendered softly. "You're right. I must."

He drew away from me and strode over to the blanketed shape in the corner. Standing between me and the light, he slowly pulled off the blanket. Hank made a sudden, overwhelming, explosive sound, like the cry of release after orgasm. That cry seemed to pull freedom itself out of its shackles, and offered liberation to me as well, as I knelt quickly and, with no caution, unbuckled the restraints that held his wrists, upper legs, and feet. His tongue went over to my hands and licked me silently, in gratitude, like a dog.

"Whoever you are, thanks," he sobbed. "Thank you, sir. Thank you!"

He was also naked, and immeasurably bigger than I had visualized him under the blanket. He must have urinated repeatedly on himself as its stiff wool was stinking with piss; and as my hands touched the thick flesh around his restraints, they felt coarse hairs covering him like a feral animal. Slowly, he stood up.

He faced me, staring, a towering giant in size and so ugly my stomach heaved a wave of nausea right up into my throat. His arms were massive, his body disfigured with boils, cuts, bruises, and warts. His belly sagged bloated, flopping over his groin, and he smelled of excrement and weeks of dried sweat.

I turned to Adam. "Who is this?"

Adam only shrugged.

"You wanted him free. I was happy to keep him under the blanket, until you left."

I nodded. "I had pity on him, that's all."

"Pity!!!" Hank exploded. "Why are you both so ashamed of me?"

He jumped lunging toward me. I tried to dodge, but he was on top of me instantly, forcing his foul breath on me. "Who are you?" he demanded to know. "Where d' you come from?"

"Perry," I answered. "From New York. I work in books—I like books—I saw Adam at the—"

"You hate me, don't you? You want t' hurt me? Kill me—"

"Hank," Adam said, smiling patiently. "If you don't watch out, I'm going to put you back in those cuffs. Now you know I can do it. So, leave Perry alone. It's obvious he's not here for you. Can't you see that?"

Hank lowered his face humbly.

"Adam, I gave you everything. Wasn't that enough?"

Adam shrugged again casually, and shook his head. I felt puzzled and repulsed at the same time. Who—or what—was this odd "room-mate," to whom Adam returned early from the baths? And had he truly given Adam everything? I looked over at the young man, but he merely looked at me with that same sweet guileless expression I had seen earlier. An expression that asked for only what you were more than willing to give, and not one drop more.

But I wanted an answer. It seemed only right that Adam should answer him. "Did he really give you *everything?*" I asked.

A tender, unexpected smile appeared on Hank's face.

Talk about *Jekyll and Hyde*, Hank looked actually more ape than man; I expected him to have a tail and claws at the ends of his huge bare feet. He had no tail, but his blackened toenails did resemble claws. He stood with his back slightly hunched over and pulled me still closer to him. I swallowed hard to keep from retching, trying to back away from his grasp, but his hands would not let go of me.

His penis, fat, repulsive, and surrounded by flesh that looked like the hairy cuticle of a horse's hoof, emerged from the concealing folds of his belly. It swung trunk-like between his thighs, revealing a dark ancient scrotum, like a rubber enema bottle pierced with bristling black hairs. These same coarse hairs grew from his chest and neck, and up into his cheeks and forehead.

"He's ashamed," Hank said, "because of what I became. I started out normal, but I gave you everything, Adam. I worshipped you like a god. I did, my beautiful friend."

Adam softly touched Hank's huge forearm, and the large creature let go of me. The young man preserved his fetching, innocent smile.

"Your *worship?* That's O.K., Hank. It's cool. But I'm tired of it, y' know? The truth is, I'm bored. There's not a lot more I can learn from somebody like you. I'm sorry, but it's the truth."

As he said that, suddenly I felt genuinely tired, and wanted to go back to Adam's room. I wanted to sleep on that mattress even in the cold, and remember this only as a dream, an upsetting one at most. I wanted to wake up later and make love to this sweet, tender young man; that was what I truly wanted, but I knew I could not leave this room.

I was mesmerized. I stood trembling from exhaustion and some insatiable, unpardonable fascination, as all I could do was watch the two of them and found myself almost as fascinated in some perverse way by Hank, as I'd been thrilled by Adam.

Hank stared at me.

"He's only bored because I'm ugly. Ain't that right, Adam? I'm disgusting?"

I started to feel colder as the morning air penetrated me, but it seemed to do nothing for them, who were both naked but were not shivering. In fact, Adam, with his pale, ivory beauty, was glowing.

"I'm bored because you no longer interest me," Adam stated. "I loved you once. You amused me. You gave me what I wanted, but that's gone."

He chuckled, folding his arms in front of himself, then turned to me, grinning.

"Maybe you'd better go. It's not pleasant here. I told you that my friends are sometimes interested in Hank. But, Perry, I don't think you're one of them. You're a book person. You're too serious. And this is real. About as real as you can get. But, in truth, I think you just see this as some other kind of story, don't you?"

I took Adam's hand; it was colder even than mine, but just having it there made me feel better.

"You're fortunate," I turned and said, shivering, to Hank, "that Adam *ever* cared for you. You're no beauty, I can see that." I started to chuckle myself. "But if Adam once loved you, wasn't that enough?"

"No," Hank answered. "Adam only cared for me because I became vile and corrupt. Right, Adam?"

Adam shook his head, as if he were admonishing a small child.

"Say any more, Hank, and I'll put you back under that blanket and have to kick you again." He turned to me and for a second I felt so close to his cool body that it seemed to warm me. "I cared for Hank out of mercy for his true self. That's the story, but it's no longer enough."

"Is that really true?" I asked Adam.

He nodded.

"Then to love anyone," I whispered to the young man, holding him closer to me, "for his true self is a gift. A real one." I wanted, out of all my past frustrations at the baths, to surrender to him. I knew that I would. "Is that," I asked him, looking into his soft golden-green eyes, "how you'll really love me?"

"Sure," Adam answered. "That's it. I knew it when I saw you at Man's Land. That was what you were looking for, and that's exactly what I can give you."

"If only you could," I said sighing, closing my eyes against a wall of feelings that were closing in on me. "If only you could; if only *anyone* could love you for what you are, what you've been through, and what you will become."

"He offers that t' everyone," Hank's raspy voice said. "It's just a come-on! He doesn't mean it. Don't listen t' him!"

"No!" Adam threatened. "Whatever you do, don't listen to Hank."

I assured him that I wouldn't and tried to pull him closer. I began crying again, maybe from exhaustion and cold, but I was trembling and couldn't seem to stop. Perhaps I was breaking down just from listening to too many stories, including my own. There was Randy who had been telling me his and trying to seduce me the way straight men did. Seduce me with attention, desirous of mine, and nothing else when you got down to it. But we want something more, don't we?

I'd wanted to crawl into Randy's seductive mouth as he talked to me; and make love to him, but I couldn't. There was no way. I'd wanted to crawl into some safety from the cold wind at the baths, but could not do that there either.

I clung to Adam's marble-cool chest and arms, until they seemed so utterly inviting as to be more apparitional than real. Then, without me being aware of it, I realized I had been passed by Adam right into Hank's reach. I looked up and saw this strange creature in front of me, with Adam only watching, smiling. That smile, the calculating frigidity of it, like he was truly offering me something, offering it to me like the beefy blonde at the baths—offering me only its absence, but I realized then, that, despite my revulsion, I had put myself in a place to receive it.

9

Hank hurled me to the cold floor and attacked me. Holding my body down with all his force, he pushed me on my stomach, pulled my legs apart, ripped my undershorts to shreds, and then using spit to lubricate himself, rammed his organ into me. I screamed, trying to push him off, screamed for Adam to come help, but he only watched from the side, with that same distant smile, as Hank hammered at me like a rag doll, punching and slapping at me until my head rang, while I tried as best I could to escape.

Finally I lay there exhausted, Hank on top of me, his bristly cheek scrubbing over my face and neck until it drew blood. I was in shock but heard him say: "Why y'want to go? Don't y'know he does this to everyone?"

"No," I cried, my eyes streaming tears.

"It's a lie," Adam said, now next to us. "Not everyone. Hank's upset. He gets his feelings torn apart. When he's working, he's O.K. He does things for me, keeps the house clean, helps with my work. Sometimes I bring him some of the men I meet. But I had no intention of bringing you to him, Perry. You came up here all on your own. Isn't that right?"

"Liar!" Hank shouted. "He would bring anyone to me. It's part of our bargain."

Adam only smiled, shrugging his beautiful shoulders.

"Is that true?" I asked.

"It's true!" Hank screamed. "Do y'think I was always like this?"

I couldn't answer, which only made him angrier and he started going at me again, forcing himself deeper, more violently inside me. I screamed for his mercy but nothing did any good; I tried to push him away but got nowhere. His revolting spit ran down my face and dribbled into my nose and mouth. I kept my eyes clenched shut, but as this monster's breathing became more intense I finally opened them and there we were: eye to eye, looking at one another, but hardly as any two, even vaguely normal human beings might.

Was he really human? Had he ever been?

His face was so twisted with anger and violence, I felt that I had come to the end of the last corridor of existence, to the very last room at the baths, the room where the most scarred, deformed, and rejected of men hung out; and there I'd found Hank. He dropped his head close to mine, then lay with his hideous face on me. I looked directly into his eyes in the thin rosiness coming from the old lamp and the window-panes now silvered with the rising light.

His eyes were close to the same intense, amber green as Adam's, but without that freshness, that frank openness of expression of the young man's. I looked directly into them as he looked into mine, and realized that I had come, up the stairs, to the third floor, only to surrender to him. I kissed him on his swollen lips and even relaxed in his arms, as he rode me like a last, broken horse that he would take with him into day-light. He did not stop, but I was no longer there. I was now fully inside myself, with that whole, marvelous, embracing multitude of books that fed me inside, that nurtured me. And, also, I must admit, with Adam, as he brought with him that atmosphere of beauty when he walked into my small room at the baths.

Finally there was Adam himself, in a pool of his own light. He watched smiling, while Hank took his pleasure from me. He was now close enough for me to touch him, and for the first time since I'd ever touched him, he was definitely warm. I could feel it, as Hank lay on top of me, violating me. Adam edged closer and I wrapped my hands, now trembling with pain, around his warm ankles. His feet slid closer, and I kissed them, feeling my tears run down them.

After this, I must have blanked out as there is only so much reserve strength left in a human being, and I had reached the end of mine. I was in a dream, swimming with Adam on a beach in the morning. We were alone, holding each other in salty water. Dolphins approached, swam around us, then the dolphins gave way to sharks.

My black-out was shattered by Hank screaming in an orgasm so loud it rattled my skull, with semen splashed on my shoulders and face, and I realized this was also Adam's, who had been satisfying himself while unconscious I clung to his feet. I was in dreadful pain, but knew I had to put some water on my face and body, cleaning myself inside and out.

Slowly, I got up and found a bathroom on the third floor, turned on an old light switch and saw more of the strange, religious pictures, some of them hundreds of years old, with lurid depictions of saints, punishments, devils, ladies, and knights. More prizes I figured from Adam's collection; I washed myself quickly then I returned to Hank's room.

He was asleep on a dirty mattress, with the same Army blanket covering him. Morning light streamed in in crystalline rays; Adam peered out the window at the street below and looked, despite the hour, more beautiful than ever. Rested, happy, he took my hand, and led me down to his room. "I'm sorry this happened," he whispered, and ran his pale fingers through my hair.

I could say nothing to him, but only looked at him.

"Is there any chance I can see you again, Perry. Make it up to you? I'll go anywhere, I promise."

I looked at his silken chest and ivory shoulders. I could not hate him, not even dislike him. How could I explain this to anyone; that I would see him again, despite him leading me into this—or had he? He was so young, innocent, and beautiful. What was he doing with this monster, who seemed to descend even beyond the horrifying borders of sadism?

In his bathroom we showered together and he toweled me off, put a mild lotion on my bruises, and I began to cry uncontrollably again.

I could not stop feeling defiled. "I feel like I've been . . . raped by the devil," I sobbed.

Adam kissed me. "I'll visit you in New York," he whispered, holding me even closer. "I'll stay with you. And you'll do things for me, you will."

I buried my face in his neck, kissing him over and over again. Yes, I thought. How wonderful that'll be, Adam without his fiendish "roommate." I would love him, I was sure of it. To have this ravishingly beautiful young man to myself; this angel with the cool skin, the soft green eyes.

PART

10

Suddenly he interrupted my thoughts. "Yes, I would like you to do things for me, Perry."

"Like what?"

"Help me with my work."

"But I thought Hank does that."

"You gave yourself to Hank, didn't you?"

I hesitated. It was hard to say this. I nodded. "I felt," I admitted, "some kind of strange compassion for him."

"Then you can, Perry, see that even Hank is human? And that it's possible to become like him?"

I nodded. Yes, I could see that.

"And you're very attracted to me, aren't you?" I nodded again. "I'm tired of Hank, Perry. So the truth is, I want you to be there for me. Do you know what I'm saying?"

"But Hank is like the devil," I protested. "Maybe more repulsive than the Devil himself. He's a monster. He won't let you go."

Adam smiled sweetly.

"Don't worry. Don't even think about Hank. He started off just like you, but got out of hand. Listen, I'll come to you in New York. Then *you* can do things for me and—"

He looked at me with that same bland lovely face, that was so child-like, and yet so suddenly, thoroughly . . . menacing.

"You're the Devil himself!" I blurted out, screaming. "I thought the Devil would be like Hank. But you're it!"

I felt so stupid; how could I have fallen into such a trap, to be seduced by such "innocence," such "guilelessness"? I was older and smarter, had lived in the world of books that I thought had saved me from the terrible shallowness of the world, from the—

"How can you say that, Perry?" he asked softly. "Let me kiss you, let me love you. Do I have the Devil's face or body? Hank has. Hank has that face and body, but me—really, Perry, how can you say something like that? I'll abandon Hank and come to you. I want you to help me, I told you that."

I didn't know what to say. We were both still naked, and it felt so nice to be there, exhausted as I was by my work and my life, in this

77

intimate way. I looked into Adam's face and realized I had never seen anyone as truly naked as he was, or as attractive in his own appeal to me. How needful, earnest, and sweet he was. He had the simplicity and earnestness of America and the world at a different time, the time of Whitman, Eakins, Housman; I could read that in his face which seemed to be covered with those magical words of desire and longing I had wanted so much to touch with my eyes and mouth. Those words created with light and the heart itself.

I drew his beautiful hand to my lips, and kissed it.

the end.

Perry Brass

An award-winning writer and gender-rights pioneer, Perry Brass has published 21 books, including poetry, novels, short fiction, science fiction, and bestselling advice books (*How to Survive Your Own Gay Life, The Manly Art of Seduction, The Manly Pursuit of Desire and Love*). An original member of the New York Gay Liberation Front, he has been involved with the movement toward lgbtq rights since 1969, shortly after the Stonewall Uprising that gave birth to the modern movement. He co-edited *Come Out!*, GLF's groundbreaking newspaper, the last three issues of which were published out of his Hell's Kitchen walk up apartment. In 1972, with two friends, he co-founded the Gay Men's Health Project Clinic, the first clinic specifically for gay men on the East Coast, still in operation today as the Callen-Lorde Community Health Service. He is a co-founder of the Rainbow Book Fair, the largest lgbtq book event in the US, and also a founder of the Gay Liberation Front Foundation, set up to foster a historical understanding of this important organization.

His work deals with issues of sexual freedom, personal authenticity, and a visionary attitude toward human sexuality coming from a life-long core involvement with the inherent value of all people. He currently lives in New York City, and can be reached through his website, www.perrybrass.com or through Facebook or Linked-In.

Other Books by Perry Brass

Sex-charge

". . . poetry at its highest voltage . . ." Marv. Shaw in Bay Area Reporter.

Sex-charge. 76 pages. $6.95. With male photos by Joe Ziolkowski. ISBN 0-9627123-0-2

Mirage

electrifying science fiction

A gay science fiction classic! An original "coming out" and coming-of-age saga, set in a distant place where gay sexuality and romance is a norm, but with a life-or-death price on it. On the tribal planet Ki, two men have been promised to each other for a lifetime. But a savage attack and a blood-chilling murder break this promise and force them to seek another world, where imbalance and lies form Reality. This is the planet known as Earth, a world they will use and escape. Finalist, 1991 Lambda Literary Award for Gay Men's Science Fiction/Fantasy. This classic work of gay science fiction fantasy is now available in its new Tenth Anniversary Edition.

"Intelligent and intriguing." Bob Satuloff in New York Native.

Mirage, Tenth Anniversary Edition. 230 pages. $12.95. ISBN 1-892149-02-8

Circles

the amazing sequel to *Mirage*

"The world Brass has created with Mirage and its sequel rivals, in complexity and wonder, such greats as C. S. Lewis and Ursula Le-Guin." Mandate Magazine, New York.

Circles. 224 pages. $11.95. ISBN 0-9627123-3-7

Out There

Stories of Private Desires. Horror. And the Afterlife.

". . . we have come to associate [horror] with slick and trashy chiller-thrillers. Perry Brass is neither. He writes very well in an elegant and easy prose that carries the reader forward pleasurably. I found this selection to be excellent." The Gay Review, Canada.

Out There. 196 pages. $10.95. ISBN 0-9627123-4-5

Albert
or The Book of Man

Third in the Mirage trilogy. In 2025 the White Christian Party has taken over America. Albert, son of Enkidu and Greeland, must find the male Earth mate who will claim his heart and allow him to return to leadership on Ki. "Brass gives us a book where lesser writers would have only a premise." Men's Style, New York.

"If you take away the plot, it has political underpinnings that are chillingly true. Brass has a genius for the future." Science Fiction Galaxies, Columbus, OH.

"Erotic suspense and action . . . a pleasurable read." Screaming Hyena Review, Melbourne, Australia.

Albert. 210 pages. $11.95. ISBN 0-9627123-5-3

Works
and Other 'Smoky George' Stories,
Expanded Edition

"Classic Brass," these stories—many set in the long-gone seventies, when, as the author says, "Gay men cruised more and networked less"—have recharged gay erotica. This Expanded Edition contains a selection of Brass's steamy poems, as well as his essay "Maybe We Should Keep the 'Porn' in Pornography."

Works. 184 pages. $9.95. ISBN 0-9627123-6-1

The Harvest

a "science/politico" novel

From today's headlines predicting human cloning comes the emergence of "vaccos"—living "corporate cadavers"—raised to be sources of human organ and tissue transplants. One exceptional vacco will escape. His survival will depend upon Chris Turner, a sexual renegade who will love him and kill to keep him alive.

"One of the Ten Best Books of 1997," Lavender Magazine, Minneapolis.

"In George Nader's Chrome, the hero dared to fall in love with a robot. In The Harvest—a vastly superior novel, Chris Turner falls in love with a vacco, Hart256043." Jesse Monteagudo, The Weekly News, Miami, Florida.

Finalist, 1997 Lambda Literary Award, Gay and Lesbian Science Fiction.

The Harvest. 216 pages. $11.95. ISBN 0-9627123-7-X

The Lover of My Soul

A Search for Ecstasy and Wisdom

Brass's first book of poetry since Sex-charge is worth the wait. Flagrantly erotic and just plain flagrant—with poems like "I Shoot the Sonovabitch Who Fires Me," "Sucking Dick Instead of Kissing," and the notorious "MTV Ab(solutely) Vac(uous) Awards, The Lover of My Soul again proves Brass's feeling that poetry must tell, astonish, and delight.

"An amazingly powerful book of poetry and prose," The Loving Brotherhood, Plainfield, NJ.

The Lover of My Soul. 100 pages. $8.95. ISBN 0-9627123-8-8

How to Survive Your Own Gay Life

An Adult Guide to Love, Sex, and Relationships

• The book for adult gay men. About sex and love, and coming out of repression; about surviving homophobic violence; about your place in a community, a relationship, and a culture. About the important psychic "gay work" and the gay tribe. About dealing with conflicts and crises, personal, professional, and financial. And, finally, about being more alive, happier, and stronger.

• "This book packs a wallop of wisdom!" Morris Kight, founder, Los Angeles Gay & Lesbian Services Center. Finalist, 1999 Lambda Literary Award in Gay and Lesbian Religion and Spirituality.

How to Survive Your Own Gay Life. 224 pages. $11.95. ISBN 0-9627123-9-6

Angel Lust

An Erotic Novel of Time Travel

Tommy Angelo and Bert Knight are in a long-term relationship. Very long—close to a millennium. Tommy and Bert are angels, but different. No wings. Sexually free. Tommy was once Thomas Jebson, a teen serf in the violent England of William the Conqueror. One evening he met a handsome knight who promised to love him for all time. Their story introduces us to gay forest men, robber barons, castles, and deep woodlands. Also, to a modern sexual underground where "gay" and "straight" mean little. To Brooklyn factory men. Street machos. New York real estate sharks. And the kind of lush erotic encounters for which Perry Brass is famous. Finalist, 2000 Lambda Literary Award, Gay and Lesbian Science Fiction.

"Brass's ability to go from seedy gay bars in New York to 11th century castles is a testament to his skill as a writer." Gay & Lesbian Review.

Angel Lust. 224 pages. $12.95. ISBN 1-892149-00-1

Warlock

A Novel of Possession

       Allen Barrow, a shy bank clerk, dresses out of discount stores and has a small penis that embarrasses him. One night at a bathhouse he meets Destry Powars—commanding, vulgar, seductive, successful—who pulls Allen into his orbit and won't let go. Destry lives in a closed, moneyed world that Allen can only glimpse through the pages of tabloids. From generations of drifters, Powars has been chosen to learn a secret language based on force, deception, and nerve. But who chose him—and what does he really want from Allen? What are Mr. Powars's dark powers? These are the mysteries that Allen will uncover in Warlock, a novel that is as paralyzing in its suspense as it is voluptuously erotic.

       Warlock. 226 pages. $12.95. ISBN 1-892149-03-6

The Substance of God

A Spiritual Thriller

       What would you do with the Substance of God, a self-regenerating material originating from Creation? The Substance can bring the dead back to life, but has a "mind" of its own. Dr. Leonard Miller, a gay bio-researcher secretly addicted to "kinky" sex, learned this after he was found mysteriously murdered in his laboratory while working alone on the Substance. Once brought back to life, Miller must find out who infiltrated his lab to kill him, how long will he have to live—and, exactly, where does life end and any Hereafter begin?

       Miller's story takes him from the underground sex scenes of New York to the all-male baths of Istanbul. It will deal with the longing for God in a techno-driven world; with the persistent attractions of religious fundamentalism; and with the fundamentals of "outsider" sexuality as both spiritual ritual and cosmic release. And Miller, the unbelieving scientist, will be driven himself to ask one more question: Is our often-censored urge toward sex and our great, undeniable urge toward a union with God . . . the same urge?

       "Perry Brass has added to the annals of gay lit." -Book Marks.

       The Substance of God. 232 pages. $13.95. ISBN: 1-892149-04-4

The Manly Art of Seduction

How to Meet, Talk to, and Become Intimate with Anyone

Winner Gold Medal Ippy Award from Independent Publisher, Gay and Lesbian Non-Fiction. "Men are not supposed to be seductive." Perry Brass proves this is not true. Always waiting for someone else to make the first move, traumatized by your fear of rejection and don't have a clue how to open a conversation or expand the terms of a relationship, then The Manly Art of Seduction is a must-have. Brass explains male territorialism, and how it keeps men locked inside themselves. He talks about making decisions yourself, and how these decisions can be used to make seduction possible—even easy. He deals with rejection, and how to use mind pictures and exercises to rejection-proof your psyche. At the end each chapter are questions you can use to tailor this book to your needs, seeing your own progress as you come to master this art.

"Relationships between men can run the gamut from brief connections to long-lasting commitments. This book demonstrates how to break through fear and old patterns to increase your seduction skills and decrease missed opportunities. No matter what kind of connection you might be looking for, the advice offered here is helpful, sharp, and pulls no punches. But the tough love is served with style and humor."

Dave Singleton, author of The Mandates: 25 Real Rules for Successful Gay Dating

"A first-class primer for every taste," Richard Labonte, BookMarks, nationally syndicated column about glbt books.

"Filled with useful, practical advice, Brass also explores deeper concepts like valor and territorialism, and his stunning chapter on rejection should be a must-read for everyone in the dating scene." Elizabeth Millard, ForeWord Reviews, Jan., 2010.

"What Brass does so well is guide a man in how to get from the initial meeting all the way to the first date and beyond. But the brilliance of the book is that you can actually read it from the perspective of the person being seduced. The "seductee" can see just how open and vulnerable the person approaching them is being, and also see what types of responses they might end up getting back. The seductee might then see himself and begin to understand how his behavior might be affecting the situation. And in that, he might learn how to let down his own guard, and allow that connection to take place."

Kevin Taft, Edge Magazine: Boston. March 1, 2010

The Manly Art of Seduction, 200 pages, $16.95, ISBN: 978-1-892149-06-0

Ebook ISBN: 978-1-892149-10-7

King of Angels

A Novel About the Genesis of Identity and Belief

Set in the haunting, enchanting landscape of Savannah, Georgia (Midnight in the Garden of Good and Evil), during the tumultuous early 1960s (the Mad Men era), King of Angels differs greatly from most novels with an lgbt theme: it is about a significant and extremely compelling relationship between a father and son—told from the bond that both father and son feel, despite differences in generation, the many secrets that separate them, and barriers of temperament but not of basic character. This nourishing father-and-son relationship is something many gay men (as well as straight men) seek, but it has been sadly missing, and missed, from most literature.

King of Angels explores this bond as part of a re-examination of the male gender and role. As Benjamin Rothberg, the half-Jewish, 12-year-old protagonist of King of Angels says about Robby Rothberg, his very tragic but heroic Jewish father, he was the "closest thing to a brother I'd ever have, even though I didn't know it then."

Finalist, Ferro-Grumley Award for Gay and Lesbian Fiction, winner Bronze Medal IPPY Award for Best Young Adult Fiction. 2012.

King of Angels, ISBN: 978-1-892149-14-5, $18.00 370 pages

The Manly Pursuit of Desire and Love

Your Guide to Life, Happiness, and Emotional and Sexual Fulfillment
In a Closed-Down World

If you are what you eat, then why aren't you what you desire? Desire stands in the great no-man's land of human activity: the zone of most conflict, fear, and anxiety. It scares us. We are often asked to hate it—by those who claim to have given it up for "better" things, and who often hypocritically haven't. Their biggest desire is power, and desire, whether you are for it or against it, is a blast furnace of power. Your desires are an opening to the world of your imagination, real feelings, and your larger Deeper Self, the Self that contains that core of your own regeneration we call the "soul." This book, a companion to Brass's The Manly Art of Seduction, is a guidebook to exploring and using your own desires without shame, but also with responsibility and maturity. This is a book about "grown-up" sex and "grown-up" feelings in an often infantile world.

The Manly Pursuit of Desire and Love, 240 pages, $16.95, ISBN: 978-1-892149-06-0

A Real Life

Like Mark Twain with Drag Queens

A Memoir. June, 1965. After a year of intimidation and persecution at the University of Georgia in Athens, 17-year-old Perry Brass hitch-hiked from his native Savannah to San Francisco, beginning an adventure he called, "like Mark Twain with drag queens." Often dead broke, he met an underground of homeless gay kids like himself, boy hustlers and the men who frequented them, as well as tormented married men, female impersonators, and ruthless cops.

A Real Life is a keyhole into being an openly gay teen in the closeted period before Stonewall, and Gay Liberation. Brass also gives an account of his abusive lesbian mother, the many jobs and "hustles" he pursued to stay alive, the beautiful teenage hustler he fell hopelessly in love with, and the older men who taught him how to live in the shadowy gay world.

A Real Life, 'Like Mark Twain with Drag Queens, 223 pages, paperback, $16.95. ISBN:978-1-892149-29-9

At your bookstore, or from:

Belhue Press
2501 Palisade Avenue, Suite A1
Bronx, NY 10463

E-mail: belhuepress@earthlink.net

Please add $3.00 shipping for the first book and $1.00 for each book thereafter. New York State residents please add 8.25% sales tax. Foreign orders in U.S. currency only.

You can now order Perry Brass's exciting books online at http://www.perrybrass.com. Please visit this website for more details, regular updates, and news of future events and books.